For the most caring and supportive family I know…
my family x

www.hazelrobinson.weebly.com

SOMETHING MISSING

BOOK ONE OF THE TRUE LOVE SERIES

HAZEL ROBINSON

Published by Little Bird Publishing House

London

ISBN: **978-1499189971**
ISBN-10**: 1499189974**

PROLOGUE

His touch was so gentle yet Susan felt it burning deep under her skin. As he caressed her stomach, she couldn't stop herself wanting him. He had completely taken over her body. The only thing she could see was the pure blue sparkle in his eyes; it was like staring at the ocean. She needed to give herself to him. She ran her hands over his shoulders and down his back, pulling him close.

There was no more pain and no sorrow. He set her free.

Susan's eyes flew open and she clutched at her chest gasping for breath. Sweat dripped down her forehead. As the nights went on, the dreams became increasingly vivid. They'd started with her decision to move to Winchelsea, and she was now beginning to wonder if it was some kind of omen. She had no idea who the man in her dream was, but the effect of the dreams was that she could feel his touch, even when awake. His kiss left its mark on her body.

Everything about him felt so real. Whoever he was, he made her feel something she could never have imagined, something she never thought she would feel.

He filled the gap where something had been missing.

CHAPTER ONE

Little ten-year-old Susan Birch stood on the grass clutching her teddy bear. Beth`s arm was wrapped around her shoulder as tears rolled down her face. Susan recognized some of the faces looking at her but some she had never met before. They each came and gave her a cuddle saying how sorry they were about her grandmother; they told her that she had been a magnificent women. They all had a story to tell.

As the coffin was lowered into the ground, Susan threw in the pink rose she had picked from her grandmother's garden that morning. Turning to Beth, she couldn't control her tears. Beth had been around Susan for most of her life; she had been her mum's best friend and so Susan had spent most of her days in Beth's house playing with her son, Max.

"Max why don't you go for a walk with Suzy?" Beth whispered cautiously.

The small boy took Susan's hand and led her off down the path whilst Beth turned to the unfamiliar women dressed in a suit.

"Lets sneak to the beech." Max laughed, dragging Susan behind him.

They stopped when they reached the sand and kicked off their shoes. Running as fast as they could, they chased each other around the beach. They had been best friends since before they could walk; they had done everything together, but now all that had changed. Max flopped to the floor, dragging Susan with him.

"I've missed you, Suzy." His elbow nudged in to her side.

Susan sat playing with the bottom of her black dress. She had lost her grandmother last week and social services came to pick her up the next day because she had no other family. They had brought her back today for the funeral but she would have to go back to the home when they came to collect her.

""I've missed you too, Max; I wish I could stay here. I asked them but they won't let me." Small tears trickled down her cheeks. "They said I could come and visit if I want to, and I can write to you."

"I hate grown-ups! I asked my mum if you could stay with us but she said they wouldn't let you. It's not fair!" Max unfastened his tie and threw it across the beach.

Susan tucked her knees up and wrapped her arms around herself. "I hate the children's home; all the other kids call me names and make fun of me."

Max curled his arm around her. "Lets run away! They can't make you go back if they can't find us. I won't let them."

"Max! Susan! Where are you?" a voice echoed from afar.

"Come on, Suzy! Lets just run away!" He stood up, grabbing hold of her hand.

"Max we can't; we'll get into trouble." Susan sunk her heels into the sand and let go of his hand.

"I. DONT. CARE!" Max stood and shouted at her.

"Max!" The voice shouted again. It was getting closer.

He grabbed her hand again. “Come on, before they find us.” But, before they could go anywhere, Beth came down the steps followed be the suited women from the funeral.

“There you both are. We’ve been looking for you everywhere!” Beth saw the tears in her son’s eyes and softened her voice, “It’s time to go now, son.” She held her hand out for him. “Susan has to go now – they have a long journey back.”

Max stood in front of Susan guarding her. “No, she doesn’t want to go back. They are mean to her! She wants to stay with us!”

Beth turned to the women and asked, “Can you give us a moment please?”

Tutting, the women nodded. “I’ll wait in my car but please be quick as we have to beat the rush-hour traffic.”

Beth took hold of Max and Susan's hand; a tear fell from her eyes. “Max, listen – Susan has to go now. There is nothing we can do; I have tried. You have to be grown up about this, son. She isn’t going back to the home, they’ve found her a family to live with.”

Max tucked himself under Beth’s arm as tears streamed down his face. “I don’t want her to go, mum.”

Susan loosened her grip from Beth’s hand. “It’s okay, Max, I have to go.” She wrapped her arms around him and she cried too.

Beth knelt on the floor in front of Susan and held her face between her hands. “Everything is going to be okay, Susan. I want you to be really brave. No more crying, okay?”

The suited women came walking back down the steps with her arms crossed over her chest. She didn’t look happy. “We need to leave now, Susan. Say goodbye!”

Susan nodded to the women and began walking. Max ran over, wrapping his arms around her, neither one wanted to let go. They had a terrible sense that they might never see each other again.

The women grabbed Susan’s arm roughly; she was getting increasingly impatient with the display of emotion. “Come on Susan, now!”

Max refused to let go. In the end Beth had to pull him away as he screamed, “No! Please don’t go, Susan. Please. Get off me! You can’t take her away!” He screamed at his mum and pulled away hard, “LET GO OF ME!”

Beth couldn’t hold onto him, her grip loosened and he ran after them. “Wait! Susan!” When he reached them, Susan turned and kissed him on the lips. It felt wet and sloppy but in a good way. Max’s cheeks went red. “Goodbye, Max,” she said, running up the steps. Max stood still. This was his first kiss, and it was to say goodbye.

Beth came up behind him. “Come on, son, let’s get you home.” She held his hand and walked him up the steps. When they reached the top, the car was driving away; Susan sat in the back waving.

On the drive, the social services lady informed her that her foster mother was a lady called Mrs. Johnson.

“She’s a very nice lady who has done fostering before. She has two daughters about the same age as you.”

Susan wasn’t convinced but was relieved when they pulled up to the house to see Mrs. Johnson standing on the door with two girls who smiled and waved in welcome. Mrs. Johnson looked friendly and Susan breathed out a sigh of relief. As she walked up the garden path, both daughters gave a polite hello and beckoned her into the house. Mrs. Johnson followed behind, talking to the social services lady.

“Susan, would you like to see your new room?” Mrs. Johnson knelt down in front of her and gave her a sympathetic smile.

Susan twisted her hair around her fingers and shook her head. “Please could you ring Beth? I said that you would ring when I got here so Max would know that I was alright.”

Mrs. Johnson stood up and smiled tightly. “You can ring them tomorrow, sweetie. It’s teatime now and we don’t want to disturb them. Why don’t you go with Nicola and Rose to see your new room?”

Susan nodded and followed the girls up the stairs and into the bedroom. The whole room was pink; the curtains, the carpet, even the beds where made up in all different shades. In the corner of the room was a small chest of drawers next to a small bed; the kind of junior bed that you have when you’re small.

"This is your bed!" one of the girls pointed to it in a snotty manner.

This is all our stuff. Don’t play with any of our stuff unless we say so!” The other pointed to the mountain of toys that had been boxed and stacked. Then they both walked out of the room, leaving Susan to unpack her small bag of belongings.

She hadn’t brought much with her, just clothes and a

few photos. Sitting on the bed, her legs tucked under, she fell into a fit of tears; she had nothing left, no family, no friends and, most of all, no Max. She didn't have many friends back home but at least she'd always had Max to play with and to make her laugh. Here she didn't have anyone. Lying down on the bed she began to drift off to sleep. She was emotionally exhausted. Through her foggy sleep, she heard the bedroom door shut and then the zip of her bag opening.

"Is this your boyfriend?" Rose bounced on the end of the bed, waving a photo of Max in front of her.

"Give that back now!" Susan shouted, springing up from the bed.

Rose jumped off the bed and passed the photo to Nicola, who ran over the other end of the room.

"Whit-woo! Kiss. Kiss. Kiss!" She laughed as she kissed the photo. "Susan has a boyfriend!"

Susan ran across the room and threw herself on Nicola, who went flying onto her back. "You're going to pay for that one, reject! I'm telling my mum." Nicola rushed downstairs with Rose hot on her tail.

Picking up the crumpled photo, Susan sat down behind the door and cried. When Mrs. Johnson tried opening the door, Susan pushed against it.

"Susan, you let me in this room right now, young lady!" Mrs. Johnson pushed as hard as she could against the door, sending Susan flying across the floor. "What do you think you are doing pushing Nicola over like that? They were only trying to be nice to you." Her hands were on her hips and she looked hard.

"But she went into my bag and took something of

mine," Susan protested. "They were teasing me and calling me names." Susan began to sob.

"We were just helping her unpack, mum, and then she flew at me and banged my head." Nicola looked up at Mrs. Johnson and fluttered her eyelashes.

"Yeah, mum, that's right – we just wanted to help her." Rose added from the doorway.

Mrs. Johnson stood looking between the girls and Susan. "Okay you two, down stairs." When the girls had gone, Mrs. Johnson turned her full attention to Susan.

"Susan, we don't accept behaviour like that in this house. I know that things haven't been easy for you, but that is no excuse for poor behavior and bad manners; you will stop in this room until you feel ready to apologise to Nicola. Do you understand?"

Susan nodded. The door slammed shut and she dived onto the bed in tears hugging the photo she had managed to rescue. When she couldn't cry anymore, she sat up and looked at the photo. It was of her and Max together in the garden. Beth had taken it a few months ago, before her world had collapsed. They stood with their arms wrapped around each other, sticking their tongues out at the camera. They were always so cheeky when they were together.

She sat on the floor and started to unpack her bag. At the bottom was a framed photo of her grandmother. She took off the back and slid in the picture of her and Max; she didn't want to face any more teasing and she was worried that the sisters might be vindictive enough to damage it. If they couldn't see it, then they couldn't tease her about it.

She sat on the edge of the bed and considered going down the stairs to apologize and get it all over with, but pride wouldn't let her and so instead she climbed into bed and pulled the covers over her head, closing her eyes and drifting off to sleep with the photo frame clutched in her hand like a security blanket. Her last waking thought was how lonely her life was going to be from this point forward.

"Susan, Susan, wake up."

Susan could hear the voice but ignoring it, she turned over and pulled herself back the covers and into sleep.

"Susan, get your lazy backside out of that bed."

Susan shook herself out of her dream and opened one eye cautiously. Sitting up on the end of the bed was her roommate, Polly, holding out a cup of coffee. They had lived together for almost six years. Polly had helped Susan re-build her life and given her not just a place to live but given her a home.

"Another one of your crazy dreams?" she asked.

"No, this was different, Pol; it was more like a memory." Susan ran her fingers through her hair and sat up, taking the cup from Polly. "It was strange – it felt so real."

Polly pulled the cover away and climbed in beside her. "What do you mean? Like you were remembering something?"

"Yeah, from when I was little. You know before all the shit happened. It was like a memory from when I was back in Winchelsea, before I left. Well, more like *when* I left." Susan jumped out of the bed and walked over to her dressing table. She reached for the framed photo of her grandmother. "I bet when I open the back of this, there is another photo – one that I'd forgotten I had," she said, fiddling with the stiff metal grippers.

Polly took the frame from her in confusion and attempted to loosen the stubborn grips. "What do you mean a photo? What of?"

Giving up, she handed it back to Susan who finally managed to pries open the back. "I mean, I hid this picture when I was about ten; when I first moved in to my first foster home. The other girls teased me about it, so I hid it. But I'd forgotten all about it until the dream I just had."

Polly took the photo and inspected it. "Who is it?"

Susan stood up and walked over to the wardrobe, "Me and Max."

"Who's Max?"

"Someone I'd given up hope of ever seeing again." Susan threw her clothes on the bed and started to dress.

"Okay, I have known you what, six years? And you have never mentioned anyone by that name, and yet you own just two photographs and he's on one of them so he must have been pretty significant."

Susan took the photo from Polly and threw it into the bag she'd pulled out from under the bed.

"It's a long story, Pol – one from a long time ago. And like I said, I'd forgotten about it until last night."

"How could you have just forgotten something like that?"

"There's a lot I've forgotten – and probably for a very good reason – to protect myself. Just leave it, please, Polly."

"No way! How long have you been having these weird memory dreams? Why haven't you said something before? Something is going on with you?"

Susan watched her reflection in the wardrobe mirror for

a moment. “I don’t know.” She shrugged. “I’ve had them for a couple of weeks, since I decided to make a return visit to Winchelsea. Last night felt so real; it was like reliving a moment in time.” Picking up her toothbrush from the sink, she threw it into her bag.

“Are you leaving today?”

Susan nodded.

Polly looked hurt. She went up to Susan and laid her hand on her shoulder. “Who is he?”

Susan breathed in deeply; even now the emotions were raw. “A long time ago he was my best friend; we were inseparable. From the age of like, two, we never went anywhere without each other. When my grandmother died he protected me from the pain. But after the funeral they came to take me away. Max wanted me to run away with him but I said no. We were just children. There was no way that we could have made it on our own.” A tear trickled down her cheek and she wiped it away with the back of her hand, embarrassed to be so emotional.

Polly threw her arms around Susan and held her in a hug. “Then what happened?”

“His mum came with the social worker. Max started shouting at them, begging them not to take me away. I told him we would still see each other. I kissed him goodbye and left in the car. That was the last time I ever saw him.”

“How old were you when this happened?” Polly had known that Susan had had a difficult childhood but she had never pried too far, fearful of pushing Susan away. She guessed that she would tell her in her own time – and now seemed to be that time.

Taking a deep breath Susan replied, “I was just ten.”

This was the first time she had opened up to Polly about anything from the time before she went into care; Polly knew almost everything that had happened to her after that, but nothing from before.

Polly cleared her throat and took the risk to ask more. “So after that you never had any contact with him?”

“Nope. When I arrived at the first foster home I asked if I could phone them but they wouldn’t let me. Then the Sisters of Evil found the picture and teased me over it. You know what happens after that.”

Polly did, and she didn’t want to drag Susan back down that road again. She lifted the photo back out of the bag and looked at it closely. Two children, so happy. Polly had never seen Susan smile and laugh like she was doing in the photo. It made her sad to think that this was now a missing part of her. “And you hid the photo so they couldn’t find it?”

“Yes, and I think over time my mind blocked it out. I suppose with everything my body was going through, my mind kept small memories safe. You know, I can hardly remember any of the happy times I had growing up, but I was ten when I left so I must have had quite a few.”

Polly placed the photo in Susan’s hand and kissed her on the forehead. “Well maybe this is all a sign. Maybe you and Max will pick up from where you left off and he will help you heal some of those wounds. Maybe all these dreams mean something.”

“Ha! What? My true love will still be waiting for me? I don’t think so; anyway he is probably married now with kids and everything. And besides I’m a little too damaged to love.”

Polly stared at her for a moment. "Don't you ever say that! I find it easy to love you. And anyway, you'll never know unless you get your ass to that train station."

Susan laughed and packed the last few items. Neither of them really wanted her to go but they both knew it would be the start Susan needed to the life she deserved.

CHAPTER TWO

Susan sat on the train and waited for her life to start again. As she stared out of the steamy window, she sank into thoughts on what her hometown would be like after 14 years away.

She was excited to be free of the hell she'd been living, but a part of her felt uneasy about the road ahead. Her life didn't have a habit of going well. As she stepped off the train, everything looked the same; everything except Susan. She was no longer the little girl who played in her Grandma's garden, or played at the beach with her friends. No, she was very different now. Life had marked her. She asked herself a hundred times if this was what she actually wanted – if this was the way to a new life, backtracking over an old one, but there was unfinished business here, stuff that she knew she had to do.

Susan jumped into a taxi and headed to her Grandma's house. Excitement built in her stomach. Her Grandma's house was her safe place, the place she always went to in her head when things were bad. It was home, and her chance to start again. To put her life on the track it should have always been on. As the taxi pulled up, she stared at the house. As hoped, it was just the same as the day she left. She paid the driver and accepted his offer of help with her bags. She took the key from the envelope she'd received from the solicitors and saw how her hand trembled as she turned the key in the lock. As soon as the door opened, she dumped her bags in the hall and ran around the house like a child. Inside, the house was different; tenants had been living in it for the past fourteen-years but moved on recently. It had been lucky timing for Susan because it had become impossible to stay in London, what with all the bad memories.

After a long weekend of receiving her new neighbours, unpacking, and getting to know the place again, Susan could not wait to get a glass of wine and settle on the sofa with her favourite book. Fortunately (or rather dangerously, depending on your perspective) the local shop and off-license was just a short walk away. She was surprised to discover the same man running it, and even more so by the fact that he recognised her immediately. He chatted to her about who had been living in the house whilst she was gone and gave her the low-down on the general town gossip, reminding her of names that she hadn't thought about for years. The more he spoke, the more she started to feel truly like she'd arrived home.

Instead of heading back to the house she went to the beach. She'd spent a lot of time wishing to walk on it again; it held so many happy memories for her. As she walked along the shore, she watched the sun setting in the distance. She thought back to the night she had discovered she had to leave. The memory was painful and she felt a tear slip down her cheek. No one could have imagined what would happen to her when she left, and no one could have stopped it. Not really. Feeling in need of that drink, she turned in the direction of home. That's when she saw him. Butterflies fluttered in her stomach as the tall, dark-haired man walk towards her.

Max had seen Susan a few times over the weekend, and he had desperately wanted to go over and say something to her, but he hadn't known what to say. When she'd walked past the garage earlier, he almost plucked up enough courage, but something had stopped him. She looked amazing, way out of his league, but he plucked up the courage now there really was no way of avoiding her.

"Hello!" he said, smiling awkwardly, and stuffing his hands deep into his pockets.

Susan blushed. She had been checking him out as he walked towards her, and had liked what she'd seen. She hadn't expected a complete stranger to actually stop and introduce himself; it certainly wouldn't have happened back in London.

"Hi!" she cleared her throat, conscious that she might be blushing, "Sorry, do I know you?" Then her eyes met his and her heart gave a little dance, *'it's him'* she thought.

"Suzy? Is that really you? What has it been? Fourteen years?"

"My name is Susan," she said warily, still unable to really associate this hot bloke in front of her with her childhood friend. She needed to be certain before making a complete idiot of herself. "Sorry, I can't quite place your name," she said coyly.

The man looked slightly hurt and replied, "It's me, Max."

She tried to calm the butterflies but they were fluttering all over her body.

"Max! I can't believe it's actually you," she said running into his arms and almost sending him flying. They began to laugh, and they laughed until tears rolled down their cheeks; but they were tears of complete joy.

They headed down the street side by side, Susan tucked her windblown hair behind her ear and caught a glimpse of Max, he was watching her every move.

"I still can't believe that it's you." Max smiled, opening the door to the bar. "When did you get back?"

Susan took her seat at the table. "Friday. I`ve moved back in to the old house."

Max ran his hand through his hair. "I still can't believe it's really you; you haven't changed a bit."

"I`ve changed more than you know, Max" she said. Her voice couldn't hide the years of sadness.

They sat and talked for hours; about their childhood and what Max had been up to during her absence. Susan felt completely at ease for the first time in a long time. Max did most of the talking, explaining about having to take over his dad's business when his dad had died. He also spoke about finishing school. Susan offered little, and what she did, she said quietly; little bits about her time growing up and school, but she wanted to keep much of herself private. Max sensed that she was hiding something but kept the thought to himself. He did not want to push her away, he was just happy to have his best friend back after so long. When Susan's grandmother had died, she'd ended up in foster care in London and he never heard anything about her again until today. He had often thought about her.

She could never have imagined the little boy chasing her around the beach would grow to be so handsome; everything about him was perfect. As she sat there, she felt a force flow between them, pulling them together; it was to strong that she didn't know how long she could fight it before doing something embarrassing.

After walking her home, Max punched Susan's number into his phone and promised to text her in the morning. He was keen to meet up and talk some more. Susan smiled, looking forward to it already. She could happily listen to him talk all day she thought as she threw her keys onto the table. With a smile on her face, she sank into the sofa with her book and the glass of wine she had promised herself three hours ago. Every page she read, she had to re-read, her thoughts were all over the place, but mainly they were about Max.

She dialed Polly's number, keen to share her news. "Pol, it's me. I've met him… I mean, Max, I've met Max and we've been for a drink and..."

Polly laughed, "Susan, hey girl, slow down. What are you on about? Who have you meet?"

Susan calmed herself down. "Max! Pol, it's Max. I met him at the beach; he wants to take me out. What do I do, Pol?"

"Okay, okay, just relax your panicking; you already know the guy so… just catch up. It's fine."

Susan flopped onto her bed. "You're right; God, I wish you were here with me."

"Susan, listen, seriously, is he hot?" she laughed.

"Hot? Polly, what? No! I mean yes! Shut up, that's not the point!"

She finished her phone-call and headed to bed; before long she was back in her dreams; she dreamt about running her hands over his chest – it was obvious he had a body built of muscle. She imagined running her fingers through his dark hair and staring in to his bright blue eyes. She woke, hot and bothered. She needed to get him out her head; she didn't need any complications in her life, not when she was just starting again. She was damaged; a relationship with Max wouldn't be good for either of them.

Susan caught sight of herself in the mirror, she looked like crap; she'd hardly slept, and when she did, her dreams were filled with Max. She knew that she should think of a way of cancelling their meeting, but she needed to see him again. Grabbing a cup of coffee, she sat in the kitchen and scoured the Internet for local jobs, occasionally jotting down a note between checking her phone. After an hour searching, she slammed the laptop shut and headed off to the bathroom.

"God you look like shit," she said to her reflection.

She needed her hair cutting and her mono-brow threading. She hated the way she looked, so she wore clothes that covered her body. She didn't want anybody to suspect the mess under her clothes. She climbed into the bathtub. When she'd finished getting ready, she checked her phone for the hundredth time.

"Still no text?" She said to the wall. "What the hell? She tucked her phone back into her pocket and slammed the door behind her before heading off to town.

Two hours in the salon and an hour in the few clothes shop and she was feeling her fresh start beginning to take place. *'Look better: feel better,'* she thought to herself lugging her bags out of the taxi; nothing would ever take her pain away but shopping sure could mask it. She left her bags in the hall and went to the kitchen to put the kettle. As she waited she pulled out her phone and cursed when she realised that it had been on silent. Her phone flashed three new messages:

Message 1: Hey! Sorry it's later than I said. Busy day at garage. Do u still want 2 meet later?

Message 2: Hey, me again. Just checking I've got right number for Suzy? Pls let me know

Message 3: Guess I'll drive by to check you're o.k

"Shit!" she said, running upstairs, grabbing her bags on the way. She threw on the first thing she could find and finished just as a knock came at the door. She brushed herself down and skipped down the stairs.

"Hey, Suzy, you okay?" He smiled. "I got worried when you didn't reply."

"Yeah, I'm fine, my phone died," she replied. "Do you want to come in?" She moved to the side to let him pass.

He nodded. "Thanks. We could still go out somewhere, if you want?"

She looked down at her leggings and baggy jumper and said, "I think in would be better, I'm not really dressed for out," she laughed.

"I think you look fine, but in is cool with me." He gave a small grin that looked decidedly flirtatious.

Max followed her in to the kitchen.

"Do you want a drink? I have beer or coffee and I think I've a bottle in the wine rack over there if you want to have a look?" She pointed to the other side of the kitchen.

"Beer is fine," Max answered, staring back at her with a smile on his face. Susan could feel her cheeks going red. He continued to look at her.

"What?" she demanded with a nervous smile.

"Nothing, I just can't believe how much you have grown up yet your still suzy, I mean you still look like Suzy. Following her into the living room, he settled in the old armchair. He wasn't trying to make her uncomfortable, but he couldn't help but watch her every move; he needed to know more about her.

Susan felt out of her depth. She could feel his eyes on her. She flicked through her DVDs nervously. "Thought we could watch a film?"

"Cool," he said still grinning.

"Sorry, I haven't had time to unpack yet." She paused, suddenly gripped by a warm burning inside. She shook the naughty thoughts away and returned to looking through the box.

"Any favourites? I'm not a massive film fan – I'm more of a book worm, so you'll have to forgive my collection." She pushed the box towards him.

"Let's see," he said, chuckling.

Looking through the box nothing really grabbed him; besides he wanted to find out more about her, not sit in silence watching a film.

"I have an idea," he said pushing the box away, "why don't we just sit and catch up; it's been so long since I've seen you and I want to know what I've missed."

Her stomach did a little turn. The things he'd missed out on weren't exactly the things she wanted to share. She hesitated, worried about what she should tell him? She didn't want him running for the door. She breathed in deeply,

"Well if we're going down memory lane then we're going to need that bottle of wine."

They sat at the kitchen table with a glass of wine. Susan began by telling Max about how she went into foster care and how the family didn't like her; she told him how the children had been cruel and called her names so that she cried night after night. She went on to tell him how the parents made her feel unwelcome, as if she were a burden, when in truth they were getting a substantial cheque from the government for their pains. They sent her to school in clothes that were too small, they refused her dinner, having had free cooked lunch at school; her uniform had never been clean and as soon as she came home, her foster parents would send her up to bed so that they could have family time together, without her. Their own children were indulged with the money that had been intended for her. In all ways she was made to feel like an outsider.

Max's smile slipped. She could feel his pity. It wasn't what she really wanted from him. She wanted to be honest with him, she wanted him to know her, but she wasn't sure that he could handle the rest of her upbringing. She drew a close under the conversation.

"So I guess that's Chapter One done with," she laughed sadly.

"Bastards," he said, shaking his head. "I can't believe you had to go through that." Susan poured them both another glass and sat back in the chair.

"I don't know what to say, Suzy. I'm sorry, I really am."

She felt warmth spread through her; it was a feeling she couldn't remember feeling since childhood. It felt a little like love. She wanted to say more, give more of herself to him, but she was frightened that he might think her too damaged.

After Max left, Susan knew nothing would be the same. He had already given her hope of the happiness she yearned for so much. She went to bed and couldn't help but smile. They had agreed to meet up the next day for a meal and to see were things went from there. Susan knew Max was looking for more than she was offering; she could tell he liked her, but he didn't know yet that she could never give him the life he wanted.

Max, on the other hand, felt very pleased with himself. From the moment he had bumped into her on the beach, he knew he wanted her more than anything in the world. He wouldn't let anything stand in his way; she was all he could think about, and he wasn't going to let her past stop him. He knew she had demons but that didn't bother him; she was stunning in everyway. His heart skipped a beat when she stepped into the room or when she looked up at him, or tucked her hair behind her ear before looking away. God he wanted her so badly.

For the first time in a long time, Susan woke up feeling amazing. She jumped out of bed with a smile on her face and went down stairs for a coffee. She sat at the table and checked her phone. There was a text from Max:

Message 1: Hey, you, just wanted to say good morning (and I'll pick you up at 5.)

Her smile turned into a big cheesy grin, which then turned into panic as she tried decided what she was going to wear. She decided to take advice and rang Polly.

After a long telephone conversation, they planned for Polly to visit in a couple of weeks, once Susan had settled in properly. With this in mind, it gave her incentive to start unpacking. She turned the stereo on and opened the nearest box; it needed to look like a home if she was going to stick around and have houseguests. She placed her books on the bookcase, and then poured herself a glass of wine whilst dancing around the kitchen like a giddy schoolgirl.

Two glasses of wine later, she found herself in the bathroom trying to do something with her hair; she settled on straightened with minimum makeup. She checked herself in the mirror and smiled. She'd changed so much in the few days she had been back at Winchelsea. A few months ago she couldn't have dreamed about getting this dressed up, let alone going out for a meal with a gorgeous, hot guy.

Thinking back to her previous life she'd had very few friends and had kept herself very private. She'd filled a lot of her time reading her angel romance books; fairy tale romances in which a fallen angel would come into her life and end all her misery. She knew that the books were filling her head with unrealistic expectations and reinforcing the idea that she would never be good enough for a happy life with the man of her dreams. She'd built a wall to stop herself from ever being hurt. She spent her days mooning over book heroes because they weren't real and could never hurt her.

Shaking herself out of her reverie, she went downstairs and discovered Max stood in her kitchen. After letting out a squeal of natural surprise and a little bit of terror, she burst out giggling.

"Sorry, I didn't mean to frighten you; I knocked, but you couldn't hear me over the music."

She felt her cheeks redden. “It’s okay, how long have you been there?”

Handing her a bunch of flowers, he smiled and replied, “Long enough to know you like singing along to Pink!” They both laughed and after a few minutes of last minute preparations, they set off out the door.

Max couldn’t believe how hot she looked in that very tight skirt; it showed nothing but revealed everything. She had the longest legs he’d ever seen, and her top was so fitted that he had a job not to stare. He’d never desired anyone as much as he desired her. He was transfixed.

Max was a complete gentleman over dinner. The restaurant was perfect; it overlooked the beach, and after their meal, Max suggested a walk along the beach. It was breathtaking; even at this time of the day the water was pure blue and the sand was warm from a day of drinking sunlight.

As they walked, Susan longed for him to take the chance and touch her, to kiss her. It was as if Max heard her desire. He turned to her, took hold of her hand, and pulled her into him. He lent down and kissed her lips softly – it was electrifying. Susan didn’t know what to do. Dropping to the floor, running her fingers through her hair she sat in silence.

“Suzy, I’m so sorry, I don’t know what came over me.” Max frowned and dropped down next to her in the sand.

“I’m not what you need, Max – please, just accept that we can’t be anything more than friends.” She stood up and wrapped her arms around herself. “You don’t know anything about me, Max. We have only just met – we’re strangers."

He crouched down in the sand in front of her, neither knowing what to say, then he cleared his throat and spoke, wiping a small tear with his thumb. "Please, Suzy, I'm sorry I kissed you"

Susan couldn't think straight, his touch had clouded her mind, it had felt beyond anything she could describe. She shouldn't feel this way about someone she hardly knew.

"It's okay, I'll walk you home."

She wanted to talk, but couldn't find the words she needed, instead they walked back to her house in silence. At the door, he turned, aware that she probably wanted some space to think things over; he went to walk towards his car but Susan shouted over to him, "Hey, don't go. Come in and have a coffee."

In the kitchen she poured them both a coffee and settled down at the table. She spoke softly, "I'm sorry about my reaction, Max, it's just that I'm not what you're looking for, trust me."

Max looked into her eyes and could see the pain

"I'm sorry, Suzy, I don't know what came over me; I just felt an instant connection with you." His head dropped and he looked at the floor. "I understand if you just want to be friends, it won't happen again." He downed the rest of his coffee and stood. He made his way to the door, but before he left, he turned and said, "That first kiss you gave me left its mark on me. I never forgot you, Suzy." He left.

Max had only been gone a few minutes but it felt like hours.

"Fuck it!" she growled, pulling out her phone to text Polly.

Poll need help. Max kissed me! I want him so much need advice xoxo

Only a few minutes passed before her phone buzzed.

Polly: bbz just go for it xoxo

She picked up her phone and sent Max a message, telling him to come back over; she needed to tell him everything and deep down she hoped he would still want her – she was ready to start her life again.

She grabbed a glass of wine and then there was a knock at the door. She braced herself for what she was about to do.

"Hey, you! Come in."

He wiped his feet on the mat and smiled curiously.

Susan waved him in and said, "Listen, I'm sorry for messing you about, but I really need talk to you. I'm going to tell you what happened to me, if that's okay."

Max made his way through to the lounge and sat down in the armchair. He could sense how serious things were and he wanted to make sure he was comfortable. She handed him a glass of wine and sat on the arm of the sofa.

"Are you sitting comfortably?" she joked, but she wasn't really trying to be funny.

Max nodded. "I want to hear this, Suzy. I want to know you."

"If you're sure."

"Yes I'm sure."

"Okay then, let me begin." She drank deeply from her glass and began. " I didn't stay at the first family house for long; it was hard work ignoring me and I became 'problematic'. They rang the social and told them that I was trouble. They said they couldn't handle me, so I was placed into the care of a young couple who had no kids. Perhaps there was a reason God had chosen not to give them children; he knew that they were evil – I mean really evil, Max; the kind of evil that you read about in the papers or see on the news. They looked like a really nice young couple on the outside but behind the gloss, they abused me in every way possible – in *every*way."

Max sat forward in his chair. He had expected it to be bad, but he hadn't guessed just how bad.

"In the end, I was rescued at the age of fourteen because they beat me so badly I had to be rushed to hospital; the authorities saw that something was terribly wrong. My foster parents had said that I had fallen down the stairs, but that didn't account for the burns or the scars that still mark me. I don't remember much about my stay in hospital, but I remember the moment they told me I had lost the baby."

Max gasped, "Oh, Suzy, I am so sorry. That's so sad."

Susan walked over to the bookshelf and pulled out a large folder. She handed it to him; inside were newspaper clippings about the case. It had been quite a news story. She was done. She left him in the lounge and went through to the kitchen to get some water. He could see her from where he sat and he saw just how broken she was. It didn't scare him. It didn't want to make him flee; he wanted to fix her.

He walked up behind her, took her in his arms and kissed her softly before letting her cry in is arms. He whispered in her ear, "I'm not going anywhere tonight, or ever, if you want me?"

He carried her into the living room and placed her on the sofa. The evening had exhausted her and she was almost asleep. He covered her with the throw and went to the kitchen to make himself a coffee. As the kettle boiled, he examined the newspaper clippings. They didn't say much about the girl, just that she had remained in hospital for several weeks before social services had came and taken her to safety. The thought of it all made him feel sick to the stomach. He couldn't read anymore. He made his coffee and switched off the light. Somehow he would have to get her to destroy them; they should not continue to define her – not anymore.

He sat in the chair and watched her sleep. She was beautiful; her thick dark curls fell over her cheek. Her lips were soft that he wanted to spend the rest of his life kissing them.

Susan woke feeling very strange. She rubbed her eyes and looked at her watch. It was 3:30am. It took her a moment to orientate herself. She saw Max fast asleep in the chair. He had stayed; she couldn't believe that after everything she had said. Her movements disturbed his sleep and he opened his eyes.

"Hey, what are you doing up? I hope you don't mind me being here, I just didn't want to leave you alone."

Susan smiled and replied, "Its fine, I'm just surprised that you stayed."

Max stood and walked over to her before wrapping his arms around her. He whispered in her ear, "I'm not leaving you – not again. I let you down when I was small. I let them take you. It's partly my fault. I'm not letting you down again." His lips brushed her cheek.

Pulling away, she looked deeply into his eyes. She knew he was true. She'd spent so long living with the thought that love would never happen for her. She took his hand and led him up the stairs.

Max pulled back for a second. "What are you doing? Are you sure about this?"

She stopped and kissed him on the cheek. "I just want you to hold me, Max. I want you to make me feel safe, and the bed is much more comfortable than the arm chair."

Max followed her into the bedroom. They lay on the bed fully clothed, curled up in the warmth of each other's bodies.

CHAPTER THREE

The next morning, Susan woke up and turned to see Max still sleeping next to her.

"It wasn't a dream," she whispered, kissing his cheek before going to the bathroom.

She stood in front of the mirror and for the first time she looked at herself and wasn't ashamed; this was the person he loved, and that's all that mattered to her. The scars that remained on her body were no longer a reminder of pain they were a reminder of the women she had become: they were a reminder that she had survived. Now, with Max by her side, she felt she could overcome almost anything.

Max smelt bacon cooking downstairs. He headed down and stood in the kitchen doorway. Susan was singing along to a song on the radio as she cooked.

"Hey you!" he said.

"Hey back at ya. Fancy some bacon?"

Max walked to the table. "Yes please."

Susan couldn't help grinning. "You got any plans for today then?" she asked, hoping that whatever they were they might involve her.

"Well actually I do; after eating my breakfast I'm going to take a shower, drive home and get changed, and then we are going out of town for the day," Max replied. He sat down at the table and Susan thought he looked right at home.

Max headed home to prepare for the day.

Once showered she flopped down on her bed and relished the feeling of being so alive. She stroked the scar on her belly. '*Somethings can't be healed so easily,*' she thought. Susan hadn't told Max the extent of her injures that resulted in her ending up in hospital on a life support machine. Deep down she feared she could never tell him.

After picking Susan up, Max drove her to the lakes. They strolled through a little park and set up their picnic. It was perfect.

"Hey, you're quiet is everything okay?" he asked, holding her in his arms.

"Yes, I'm fine. It's just all a little overwhelming," Susan replied.

"You can talk to me you know, Suzy. Haven't I proved that already? Nothing you tell me will get rid of me; you're stuck with me now and forever." He spoke softly into her ear and little goose bumps travelled up her arms.

"It's just all so new to me; this doesn't happen to me, and I don't really know how to act."

They spent the afternoon walking around the lake before driving back to Susan's. It had been a truly perfect day, and Susan couldn't help dreaming of a life where they did this every weekend until they were old and grey and full of family stories.

"I need to go home for a bit," he said. "I've got some paperwork to do. Do you want me to come back later?"

She nodded. Everything was moving so fast, but it felt right. "Yeah, that would be good. I can cook us dinner if you want?" Susan said as she climbed out of the car.

Max flashed her a smile. “Great! Want me to bring anything?”

“Just you will be perfect.” She winked at him. She waved him off as he beeped his horn.

Tonight was going to be perfect.

There was a playful tap at the door before Max walked in with the biggest bunch of flowers she’d ever seen.

Max pulled her in for a hug, squashing some of the flowers between them and causing their scent to drift.

“These are lovely, thank you! Drink?”

Max followed her lead into the kitchen where dinner was in full production. “You have been busy!” His eyes roamed up and down her body, admiring the dress she’d picked out.

“Is this all this for me?”

Susan nodded and poured out the wine before checking in on the dinner.

After dinner, Max took Susan’s hand and led her to the sitting room. Placing his arm around her waist, he led her slowly in time to the music. She looked stunning. The deep purple silk wrapped around her breasts enticingly. He thought about kissing her hard, and pushing her back onto the sofa – but he knew, despite his mounting passion, he would have to take things slowly; win her trust.

He stroked the back of her neck and she dropped her head onto his shoulder. He let his hand roam down her back and kissed her neck. The bristles on his chin tickled her. She yawned. It had been a long, exhausting couple of days.

“Tired?” he whispered.

She nodded.

"Bed?"

She smiled and nodded again. He flicked off the stereo, killed the lights and led her up to bed.

They lay on the bed and she lay in his arms. There was an unsaid understanding that this wasn't a straightforward, 'normal' situation.

"Is it okay if I stroke you?" he asked.

She looked at him hard and nodded her head. As he stroked the scar on her stomach, Susan's body flinched at his touch. "Why do you flinch when I touch you there, Suzy?"

"Not tonight, Max. Some scars can't heal. I don't want to talk about it now." She pulled him in for a kiss.

Susan felt completely safe and dared to wonder if this was what her life was going to be like from now on with Max by her side. She pictured them old and grey sitting in the garden.

"Max," she whispered, "please do something for me?" She looked deep into his eyes.

Stroking her hair he replied, "Anything, Suzy."

"Please don't call me Suzy. I'm not that person anymore."

Confused he just stared at her.

"He, the man that did this to me, used to call me Suzy. Before I came here, no one called me that but him."

"I had no idea. I'm sorry… Susan."

"You weren't to know, it's just that I don't want to think about that when I'm with you." He held her whilst she drifted off to sleep.

Next morning, Max asked if she'd like to meet his mother. Her first thought was say no, but he'd done so much for her, and if this was the beginning of their life together, she needed to try and do it properly.

As he parked the car in the drive, Susan's nerves kicked in.

"What if she doesn't like me?" she asked nervously.

He reached over and took her chin. "You, my love, have nothing to worry about; she has been dying to meet you since I mentioned you were home the other day." He gave her a small kiss on the side of her cheek before getting out of the car.

As they approached the door, Max's mother, Beth, came running from the door with her arms spread wide with intention of wrapping Susan in a big embrace. "Susan I'm so happy to finally see you again after all these years."

"You remember me?"

Beth smiled. "Of course I remember you! We could never get you to leave our house."

With a giggle they all went in to have lunch.

When they arrived back at Susan's, she reached for him and pulled his hands around her waist. She had made a decision that afternoon. Sitting in Beth's kitchen and looking at the family photos of Max as a little boy, she realized that she wanted to live a normal, happy life with Max. She wanted to have a family, and she wanted to make right the things that had gone wrong. There were ways around the physical barriers, and she knew that with Max in her life, they could do the impossible. She leaned in and pressed her lips onto his. For a moment, the earth stood still. Nothing existed but the two of them.

"What's that for?" he asked.

"I don't know, it just felt… right. I want to see were we can take this," she said, taking hold of his hand. She led him into the hallway and then up the stairs. Max was unsure she was ready for this, but he wanted every part of her so badly that he pushed his concerns aside and followed her lead; this was the decision he had made. Susan wondered if she should have perhaps had a glass of wine or two, to help her stop the thinking. It was the thinking that did the damage. She knew she wanted to do this; she needed to do it. Finally, she wanted to be free from all the bad associations attached to intimacy, and love. She sat on the edge of the bed, and fought back tears.

Max looked at her and bit down on his lip. "Please don't cry. You don't have to do anything you don't want to. I don't want to push you into anything. There's no rush, I've waited years for you."

"I want to make love with you," she said. "I need to break free from the fear." Most of my life I've been broken; I never thought I would feel again – and then you came along. The moment I met you I knew everything had changed."

He stroked her soft, dark curls. Her lips quivered with his touch. Taking his time, he undressed her. Susan's body trembled at his touch, but it wasn't fear or shame, this was soft and sensual. Max slowly laid sweet, undivided kisses on every inch of her broken and scared body, giving her time. Slowly his hand moved up and down over her hips. He kissed the nape of her neck and sent shivers of desire through her.

"Max," she groaned from deep within.

"Do you want me to stop?"

"No." It was as though her body called for him.

Max's hands moved over her breasts, making small concentric circles, "Max," she groaned again.

He laid her down on the bed, coaxing her body to respond. He paused and looked deep into her eyes, asking permission.

She nodded, pulling his hips towards her.

Susan cried out in pleasure, tilting her head back. She mirrored his movements until Max gripped her thighs as his body stiffened.

"Oh God, Susan…God, you're so perfect!" he groaned with pleasure.

Max pulled Susan to him and cuddled her close. Lying side by side, she rested her head on his chest and caressed her back.

"Are you okay?" he whispered into her ear.

"I'm good!" She closed her eyes, soaking in every delicious memory of him.

"Are we moving to fast Max? I mean don't you feel a little like we are in overdrive?"

He lifted her chin up and locked eyes with hers. "Honey, every minute with you is a blessing, and when I'm not with you, I can't stop thinking about you."

"Max, the feelings I have for you are so familiar; it's like they were always there. I know it's all happening too quickly... I can't... My head keeps telling me to slow down."

Max kissed her softly and placed his hand on her chest,

above her heart. “What does your heart say, baby?”

His hand felt warm and his touch made her heart beat. “I… I don’t know it beats too fast when you’re around.”

Max brushed his hand down her chest. “That’s just how I feel. Susan, I love you. I don't care how fast we are going, it’s not going to change.” He placed her free hand on his chest and she felt his heart racing as fast as hers.

“Oh, Max, I love you too!” I know now I always have,” she whispered. His mouth traced her neckline, and he held her breast in the cup of his hand.

“Max...” she gasped. Her head tilted back at his touch.

He made love to her again, and this time it wasn’t full of worry, and doubts, and anxieties. This time she gave herself completely to him. The burn on the inside wanted out, and she let herself fall into ecstasy. Her whole body trembled.

Max whispered into her ear, “Come away with me, Susan!”

CHAPTER FOUR

Two weeks later

'*Come away with me, Susan,*' turned into him booking a weekend away in Paris at the Hotel Regina, near to the Louvre. Susan had always wanted to visit the gallery and walk along the Tuileries, floating sailing boats on the fountain and drinking coffee on little rattan chairs, watching life go by.

They spent the whole weekend talking about their future together, fantasizing about a little cottage and children playing in the garden; only Susan knew that it was a dream that would most likely never happen; she still had doubts about their future because she was still keeping her biggest secret from him: the fact that she could never be a mother. And the thought made her desperately sad, because to have a family with Max was something she wanted more than anything else in the world.

After lunch, at which they sank a couple of bottles of wine without realizing, they couldn't wait to get back to the hotel room and play. Max had blown the budget and got a suite with a sunken Jacuzzi that just begged to be used.

"Bit too much bubble bath there, sweetheart?" Max giggled, as the bubbles started to spill over the top.

Susan threw a handful his way before saying, "You could come over and join me. There's room for two!"

A boyish grin spread over his lips. "I thought you'd never ask," he said, already undoing his buttons.

Max had seen Susan naked many times since their first night, but not like this. In his eyes, she looked like a goddess. He got in and she turned around, spooning herself between his legs so that he could rub her back. He pushed her hair over her shoulder, exposing her perfect neck and noticed a cluster of scars just beneath her hairline. He hadn't noticed them before. He stroked them with his fingers and Susan arched her back and wiggled her shoulders.

"They're from cigarette burns," she said softly.

Unsure what to say, Max softly covered them in kisses. There was still so much he didn't know about her. Each time he was with her, he discovered a little more.

"Susan, do you trust me?" Max asked, kissing her shoulders.

She turned to him, curious about such a question. "Of course I trust you – what makes you think otherwise?"

He took her hands and kissed each of them softly. "I want you to tell me everything; I want there to be nothing between us. I want you to love yourself as much as I love you. I know it's painful talking about it, but I think if we talk about it, and it's out in the open, you don't have to ever think about it on the inside again."

He felt Susan tremble under his touch. She shrugged and took in a deep breath. "I don't know, Max; I tried talking about it during therapy – years of therapy, and talking about it didn't seem to do much good."

"But they didn't love you like I do. They weren't with you, by your side."

She shrugged, "I don't know, Max. Can we see how it goes?"

"Of course. Stop if it hurts too much."

She took in a deep breath and took a hold of his fingers, placing them on scars at the bottom of her leg. "Punishment for crying." She spoke so softly Max could barely hear her.

"And these?" he asked, gently, pointing to three silver circles by her knee.

"A warning not to tell anyone." A tear trickled down her cheek.

"And these?" he whispered, as he inspected the tiny marks at the top of her arm.

"When I stared my period he told me things was different. When I wouldn't play with him, he branded me." Susan spoke with anger in her voice.

Max's muscles tensed with anger. He began to think that the whole sharing thing wasn't such a good idea after all.

"And this?" he asked, his voice thick with pain.

He felt Susan shudder in his arms. She was crying. "I'm sorry, I can't. I can't share her. She was mine, Max. My only hope in a dark world and she was taken from me."

*

She was dressing for dinner when he came up behind her and presented her with a small velvet box. "I have a gift for you," he said.

She opened it and saw the most beautiful thing she'd ever seen; a white gold chain with a red ruby heart wrapped in two-angel wings.

"I want you to wear this forever, Susan. It's to remind you that my heart and soul are always with you; they belong to you now, and always will." He placed the necklace around her neck. "The heart represents your heart, and the wings are my arms – I'll never let go."

Her fingers touched the heart. "I'll never take it off. I love you so much."

"Do you think we will always have this time together?"

Susan turned her head and looked at him. "I hope so."

His eyes twinkled. "Me too. Just imagine me, you and a couple of little ones running around."

Susan stiffened. "I… I don't know. Do you want kids?"

"Susan, I want everything with you."

They sat the next morning at breakfast, surrounded by Parisian grandeur. She knew that she had to tell him about the fact she couldn't have children. She couldn't let him keep dreaming about a future that wouldn't be; it wasn't fair. She was just about to do it when the waitress interrupted them. 'Fate' she thought, and was relieved to leave it until they got home.

Walking around the Louvre, she clutched the necklace. Last night they had come back from dinner and made love and it was the first time that it had felt like he wasn't trying to fix her. It had felt like the first night of their new lives together. It had been heavenly and she worried that if she told him the truth she might never taste heaven again.

That night as Susan lay beside him she memorized every inch of his body; his thick brown hair, his dazzling blue eyes, his soft lips – she needed to store them in case this was the last time she was with him. His body was her idea of total perfection. If she didn't tell him about her inability to have children then she could keep him forever, but she knew that would only make them both unhappy in the end.

The flight home was quiet. Max had tried talking to her but she'd put her walls up around herself. Her heart was breaking. By the time the taxi pulled up outside her house, she was starting to lose her mind at the thought of losing him.

Max took her by the hand and led her into the house. He put the kettle on and cleared his throat before speaking.

"Susan, I've been thinking and we need to talk."

Susan's heart jumped into her chest. She was confused – was he going to break up with her? She sat down at the table. "I was thinking the same thing, can we just sit for a minute?" she said.

"This weekend has been amazing…"

"...but?" Susan asked, dreading his answer.

"But nothing!" he said raising an eyebrow "And... it has made me realize that I never want to be apart from you. Soooo… I was thinking that maybe I could move my stuff in here?" He blushed, mistaking her silence for uncertainty, "I'm here most of the time anyway, and I really think it's about time we made the next step."

Tears started to stream down her face. "Max, I really don't think that is a good idea, I don't want you to move in. In fact, I think we should stop seeing each other."

Max's face dropped. "What are you talking about? I don't understand. I thought we were happy?"

"We are – at the minute, we are! But, Max, listen to me, I can't give you the future you want. I won't let you settle for second best. There's someone out there that can give you everything you want: someone who can give you children."

"I don't understand. It's you I want, nothing else matters."

"You think now that this is all perfect, but what happens when you want more? What happens when you want children? I can't have children; I had my chance and *he* took that away from me. He made sure I would always suffer at his hand." She started to sob, and not wanting him to see her like this, not wanting him to stop from leaving, she fled to the bathroom.

Max stood in the kitchen trying to take everything in. He was suffering severe whiplash – he hadn't quite known what to expect from his proposal but it certainly hadn't been this. He ran up the stairs after her, and slumped down outside the bathroom door. He was crying – something he hadn't done since being a child.

"Susan, please talk to me. I don't want to lose you – please!"

"Just go, please. I'll never be enough for you, just go!"

Max filled with anger – he wanted to kill the bastard who had done this to her.

"How can you say you're not enough for me? You are my life. You swept me away the moment our eyes met. When I'm with you, the whole world fades away, and all I see is you; when you fall asleep in my arms, I stay awake just to watch you breathe. Susan, I can't get enough of you: you are more than I could ever need." He stood and lent his head against the door. "I told you, you have my heart and soul, and always will."

Susan heard his footsteps fade and all she could do was cry.

When she could cry no more, she stood up and opened the door; she felt sick from the pain. She headed downstairs to get a drink of water. When she got to the kitchen, she found an envelope on the table. She sat down and opened it inside was a letter.

Susan, my love,

Words can't describe how I feel about you. The moment I met you, I knew it was love.

And you think that you wouldn't be enough for me; you think that you are weak, but you are wrong – you complete me. You are the strongest person I know. I love you and always will. You thought I was your angel, but I think you're mine. If you love me as much as you say you do, please meet me at our place at midnight.

Ill be waiting for you,

All my love,

Max x

Susan's whole world came crashing down around her; she had to leave before she gave in and went to meet him. Polly would help her through this. She went upstairs and packed before writing a note for him. If she were gone, he would have to move on. She took off the necklace and placed it in the envelope along with the note. It was 11:50; he would already be at the beach – waiting for her.

Back at the beach, Max sat in their spot for over an hour. He couldn't believe she thought he would love her less if she couldn't have children; he was happy just to have her – he didn't need anything else – and besides, there were other options; other people got around it, and he was sure they would too. Eventually he got up, but he wasn't prepared to give up. He walked to her house, but when the lights weren't on and she didn't answer the door, all he could do was head home.

Beth was sat on the doorstep holding an envelope in her hand. "Max, she's gone." "She called by and left this for you." Beth handed him the letter and headed inside – he needed his space.

My dearest Max

I can't thank you enough for the happiness you have given me. You are the love of my life and always will be, but I can't stay. You will only end up regretting being with me. Because of this, I have to leave. Please don't try looking for me; when you're around my heart leads the way and I know in my mind I'm not enough.

You told me my heart is held in your arms – well that is where my heart will stay. I know it will be safe with you.

I never thought I could be loved but you gave me that gift, and I am so thankful. I can go on in life knowing this. You have given me hope.

I will always love you, Max

Goodbye,

Susan x

CHAPTER FIVE

As Susan arrived at Polly's flat, she breathed in deeply and knocked. Even though it was the early hours of the morning, her friend opened the door and ushered her in with a massive hug. "Oh my God, Susan, what is it? What's happened?"

"I really needed to see my friend."

"Oh, Susan! Come in, it's late; we'll talk in the morning. You know where your room is. Susan was so exhausted that she fell straight to sleep as soon as her head hit the pillow. She might have left Max behind but he was still in her dreams. She knew that she would never escape them.

The sound of Polly pottering around in the kitchen, woke her.

Polly was the only other person she had told about the full horrors of her experience. It had been Polly who had helped her through it all, even going to the psychologist with her at the start. But Susan couldn't open up to them.

When they had met, Susan was a mess. She had started drinking to numb the pain and Polly became her sponsor, giving her a place to stay and helping her get a job – Polly had given Susan the precious gift of normalcy. When Susan had moved away Polly thought that it would finally free Susan from her demons, but she had been wrong and now she felt terribly responsible.

"Hey, you ready to talk to me now?" Polly asked as she placed a cup in front of her friend.

"Not really," Susan replied. She wasn't ready for her friend to tell her what a fool she'd been. She already knew that.

"So when then, Susan? When you hit the bottle again and I'm pulling you out of the gutter? Or when you try taking a load of pills again? You know you need to talk to me about this. You told me everything was fine, so what has happened? You can't just turn up here middle of the night and collapse on the doorstep. NOW TALK!"

"Alright, I ended it. Happy now?" she said slamming her cup down on the table.

Polly's face changed. "What do you mean, you ended it?"

"I think I made a big mistake, Poll, and I don't know what to do." Susan held her head in her hands and cried.

Polly walked over to her and pulled her head up. "You silly women; you didn't think he would want you did you? Has it never occurred to you that someone out there loves you more than anything in the world, and you are too scared to let yourself be happy? You're scared of someone wanting you, aren't you? You think you don't deserve love, but you do. More than anyone I know."

Polly was right but deep down Susan knew it wasn't as simple as that. She knew that Max alone wasn't enough for her, she wanted his children, and she wanted to sit in the garden with her husband with their children running around them. If she could only have half of that dream, it wasn't enough.

"Polly what have I done?" she asked, clutching his letter in her hand.

"Even after you told him, he still wanted you; wasn't that enough for you? You need to sort yourself out; get rid of all that crap that's floating round in your head and get him back." Although Polly said this like it was simple, she knew it was far from it.

"Go and have a shower and then we will work out a plan." Polly wasn't asking now, she was telling, and all Susan could do was obey.

When she left for the shower Polly went through

Susan's bag and found her phone. Any guilt she felt about raiding her friend's bag was drowned out with good intention; she needed to sort it out. Polly scrolled through the texts and found Beth's number. She had contemplated phoning Max but guessed somebody important enough for Susan to ring might know something.

Polly spoke with Beth for a couple of minutes before deciding that it would be best if they met up in person. She left a note for Susan on the kitchen table. After the two-hour drive, Polly arrived at a small café, where they arranged to meet sitting in a booth at the back was a women wearing a blue coat. She walked over to the booth. "Beth?" the women turned round and gave a worried smile.

Polly could tell that Beth was heart-broken over Susan leaving. They sat and chatted for a while, mainly about Susan's childhood and how Beth had cared for her. Polly explained why she had come and what she hoped from meeting with Beth,

"I don't know, it may take a while but I think if Susan can empty the rubbish in her head she'll realize that she's meant to be with Max," she explained.

Beth gave a little smile. "I hope you're right; we both love her so much. I just want to see her happy and safe. I feel like I let her down before and I'm not going to this time." Beth had felt years of guilt, thinking she could have done more to help Susan. There wasn't a day go by when she wished she could turn back the clock and be brave enough to have taken her in. She would never forgive herself if anything happened to her this time.

Polly grabbed Beth's hands. "Listen, I met her when she was at her worst; she was nineteen and in a bad way. I really didn't think I could help her but she pulled through. I know she was happy with you and Max in her life. She rang me the other week and told me what you tried doing for her; you could not have done anymore."

Beth didn't know what to say. The two of them hugged

and Polly asked her to give Max a message from her – not to give up hope and that she would make sure Susan was back with him soon.

Beth's drive home was full of hope that everything would work out. When she got home she went upstairs to see Max but he wasn't in his room. She headed down to the beach, knowing that this was where he went to think. She saw his silhouette on the beach and headed towards him.

"Why did she do it, mum? Why did she go?" His voice was tired and croaky.

Beth put a hand on her son's arm. "Max, her friend rang me and I went to meet her…" before she could carry on Max interrupted her.

"What do you mean? Where is she? I'll go and get her. I need to speak to her?" Max was ready to go. He didn't care how far away she was, he just wanted her back.

"Max, listen, Polly said she's in a bad way; she said she would be able to help her. However, we need to leave her to it for a while. She told me to tell you not to give up. She hopes she will have Susan back with us soon. We just need to give her space for a while."

Max was angry; he could have helped her, he wanted to be the one to take care of her, not someone else. "What? So I'm meant to just sit and wait? I don't think so mum. I only just found her I'm not losing her again. I'm not the kid anymore." He was already walking back to the house and Beth trailed behind him. She understood her son's desire to fix Susan – she felt it herself, but he needed to realize that Susan was fragile, and his needs didn't come into it – he risked damaging her further.

"Listen to me, we need to let Polly get through to her first; leave it a few days, please, for me. I want her back just as much as you do, but she needs to deal with her problems first. If you go over there now you will only push her further away."

Max knew she was right, his mother most often was.

He jumped in the car and headed for Jessop's snooker house and bar for a beer. He spent most of his weekends playing snooker with his friends, before he met Susan that was. He felt the need to have a few drinks and see if any of the lads wanted a game.

The minute Polly had left the house, Susan hit the bottle of wine. She spent all afternoon on the sofa with her glass, listening to music. It was the only way she knew how to numb the pain. She kept checking her phone but there was nothing, only another empty glass. Just then the door opened and Polly walked in. She grabbed the glass from Susan's hand.

"Oh no you don't – we're not going through all that again. It didn't work the first time and its not going to work now." She stomped into the kitchen and poured the remains of the bottle down the drain, more for effect than purpose. She put the kettle on. "You need to drink some coffee and start explaining."

The only thing Susan wanted to do was drink and sleep. Polly handed her a cup of coffee and sat down next to her.

"We need to sort this, Susan. You're not going to find the answer at the bottom of the bottle and you know that. Only you can put this right." She stroked Susan's hair away from she face. "Talk to me, please."

Susan took a deep breath. "I don't know how to fix it Poll. How can I put it right? I thought I could walk away from him; I thought it was the right thing to do, but I was wrong. Am I being selfish wanting him to give up the chance of a family for me?"

Polly knew the answer, "Of course you're not selfish. What would give you that idea? I know he loves you, and you deserve to be loved, but if you keep thinking like this you will never be able to let him into you life. You need to get rid of this stupid idea that a child would make you both happy and somehow love each other more. It isn't the answer. I know you want to be a mum, but he wants to love you for a lifetime. Which is more important to you?"

Susan knew Polly was right. She had so badly wanted to be a mother that she had convinced herself it was what he wanted too. Did he secretly know her suffering?

"You're right, Polly but its too late, I have smashed everything to pieces and I can't put it back together. I have taken the best thing to happen to me and thrown it away. How do I fix that?"

Max headed to bed, heavy hearted that it would be alone. Before switching off the light, he checked his phone and noticed a missed call from Susan. He wanted to call her back straight away but reminded himself that she needed time, he couldn't help her in the way she needed. He looked at the picture of her on his phone. It was taken in Paris on the hotel balcony. She looked so happy and peaceful. It had been the night he had given her the necklace. All along she had been planning on ending it. How could he not have seen it?

Polly sat on the sofa with a very serious look on her face. "I need to ask you something and I don't want you to go of the rails. I know you're not going to like it."

Susan nodded. She trusted Polly with her life – literally.

"I've been thinking about things – a lot, and I've got some questions that I think we need to explore, but it means that we are going to have to go back over some painful memories. Are you in a place to do that?

Susan nodded her head tentatively, thinking that she hurt so badly already that surely nothing else could hurt more.

Polly paused, selecting her question carefully. "When you lost the baby, who told you that you wouldn't be able to have children?

Susan jumped from the sofa. "Why? Why do you need

to know that?"

"Susan, calm down and listen to me. Did any of the doctors actually tell you, in exact terms that you wouldn't be able to have children in the future?"

Susan went to say something but lost her words. She was angry and upset. In the end she shrugged her shoulder violently and fought off tears.

Polly hesitated, "… or was it him? Did he tell you that?"

Susan's memory flashed back to that afternoon in the hospital and the image of him leaning in close to her ear, hissing threats and telling her that she deserved everything that had happened to her. He told her God was punishing her for her sins and that he would never let a little slut like her be a mother.

She felt the beginnings of a panic attack. It was all too much; she couldn't think about all that now.

CHAPTER SIX

Polly knocked on the door several times throughout the day, but each time Susan told her to go away and leave her alone. She hadn't eaten or drank all day. Every inch of her body ached for Max. He still hadn't returned her call.

The move had meant to be a fresh start but instead she'd just ended up back at the start; here in Polly's apartment, depressed, hurt, and alone. She picked up her phone and tried ringing him but no one picked up. She sent him another message. She waited for a couple of hours. She desperately needed a drink. She needed to lose herself.

She found herself sat at the bar in a sleazy club.

"Allow me," the man next to her said. "I'm Dean."

"Susan," She answered

"Fancy a dance?" he asked leaning over to her and placing his hand on her knee.

Susan nodded and let him lead her onto the dance floor.

His hands were tight around her waist, and he was kissing the nape of her neck. The drink, the lights and the movement all created a dizzying effect. He spoke into her ear, "Do you want to get out of here?"

Susan nodded. Alcohol had taken over her rational mind.

"I don't usually do this you know," Susan said shyly.

As the entered Dean's flat, he was all over her, kissing the nape of her neck, stroking his hands over her breasts, unzipping her skirt. There was no time to think. She kissed him back, hard. Undid the buttons of his shirt. He picked her up and carried her to the bed.

There was no tenderness, no love. It was a drunken fumble with no pleasure, just a series of sensations.

As Dean slept, she went to the bathroom and looked in the mirror. Guilt overwhelmed her. How could she do this to him? She had let him down in every way possible. Her head was pounding from the drink and her heart was breaking over the thought of Max at home alone.

She rushed into the bedroom, threw on her clothes, and headed out the door, grabbing a half filled bottle of Vodka from the kitchen top as she went.

Before she knew what was happening, she was sitting in the park having succeeded in losing herself.

CHAPTER SEVEN

The morning sun poured through the curtains. Susan struggled to open her eyes. She could not remember how she got home but she could remember her night being full of dreams of Max. She remembered storming out on Polly and then everything went blank.

Wrapping the cover around herself she headed into the kitchen. That was when she saw him standing in Polly's kitchen with a cup of coffee in hand and the other held in greeting.

"Hey," he said.

"Hey," she replied, still not certain that she wasn't dreaming.

"You gave us all a real scare last night you know."

She blushed and pulled at the cover. Max handed her his cup of coffee, and she took it smiling.

He reached out and pushed a tangle of hair away from her face.

"Polly phoned me," he offered as way of explanation.

"Oh," she said.

Polly walked in through the front door, carrying a loaf of bread. "Oh, you're up."

Susan looked at them both. They'd gone to so much trouble to make sure she was safe. It was at that moment she realised what family really meant. This was the only family Susan needed. With them around she knew they would get her through anything.

Polly ran Susan a bath and walked her to the bathroom.

Susan's legs still felt like jelly from all the shock. "Please don't leave me," she said grabbing Polly's arm. She shut the door and helped Susan get out of her clothes before helping her into the bath.

"Susan, last night, we were so worried, what happened?" she said washing Susan's back.

Susan tucked her legs under her chin and cried. "I don't know, I felt like I couldn't think straight anymore."

"Oh, sweetheart, I wish I could take it all away for you."

"I want Max to take me home – do you think he'll do that?"

Polly gave a smile as she helped Susan out the bath. Go and get dressed and I'll talk to him. As they came out the bathroom, they could hear Max on the phone to Beth. "I think Susan should see a doctor. I'm really not sure I give her the help she needs."

Susan's face crumpled in pain. She let go of Polly's hand and ran back into the bathroom, locking the door behind her. The sound of the door slamming caused Max to look up the stairs and see Polly standing open mouthed. She shook her head and Max came bounding up the stairs. He knocked on the door.

"Go away," Susan shouted. "I'm sorry I'm such a burden on you, Max. You can leave now, you have done your hero bit."

"Susan, please, listen, I didn't mean that how it sounded. Please, just open the door and let me in." Max felt helpless. "Please, we have been here before and neither of us wants to make the same mistake again."

There was a moment of silence and then the sound of

the lock sliding open.

He found her sitting on the floor all curled up, tears streamed down her face. He sat down on the floor next to her.

"I searched for hours for you. When I found you in the park I was worried sick, you looked so ill. I never want to feel like that again, I never want to feel like I'm too late, but I don't know how to help you deal with this. I'm not sure that I'm strong enough – and that isn't your fault, it's mine. But that doesn't mean I'm giving up on you."

Susan lifted her head and looked at him. She could see in his eyes that he must have spent the whole night awake, making sure she was okay. How could she have got things so wrong? She had let fear takeover her life.

He held out his hands and folded hers in his. "Baby, I promise you I will never turn my back on you."

"This is all my fault. I thought it would be better but I just ended it but I…"

"Ssh, don't worry about any of that now. Come home, Susan. We'll get help and we'll get through it together." He moved closer, teasing her lips with his before kissing her long and deep.

She breathed in every part of Max's body and ran her fingers up his chest their eyes locked as he pushed her hair behind her, his fingers ran through her curls.

"I guess you too have made up then," Polly said from the door. "Sorry to interrupt but your mum is on my phone for you."

Whilst Max spoke to Beth, updating her on the situation, Polly followed Susan through to the guest room and watched her pack.

"If you're going back, I'm coming with you. Max has said it's okay."

"What do you mean you're coming too?"

"Well I hate my job, I live in a tiny apartment that I rent at vast expense and I keep bumping into my shitty ex, so I mean I am coming with you and renting out Beth's spare room for a few months."

"I can't ask you to do that. I can't expect you to give up you life here to babysit me again." Susan knew that wasn't the only reason Polly was doing it, but she couldn't expect her to drop everything for her – not again.

Polly laughed, "Oh please, honey, I won't be doing any babysitting that's what you have Max for. It's just that I want to be around to help, and besides, I missed you when you were gone." They shared a long hug.

Susan went to the door and checked the hallway, making sure Max wasn't around. She closed it and turned up the radio just to make sure she wouldn't be overheard. "I wanted to talk to you to before I spoke to Max," she said in a low voice.

"What is it?" Polly asked.

"Don't look so worried, it's nothing bad. I want your advice."

"Okay," she said nervously.

"Well I've decided that I don't want to see anyone about children; I don't want to know what my options would be. I don't want to know how damaged, or not damaged I am. I don't want to be poked and prodded and gawped at."

"But being informed would be really positive, Susan."

Susan shook her head. “Look, I don’t want to go and be told it’s true or not true. I’m going to try, and if it doesn’t happen, then we’ll deal with it.” She twiddled her hair nervously.

“If you are you sure that’s what you want?” Polly smiled tightly. “And if it doesn’t work, can you really cope with that?”

“Yes, I’m sure. Max will be with me. All I can do is try.”

They returned home, and went to bed where they made love slowly and tenderly. As she lay next to Max she knew she wanted to spend the rest of her life with him. She wanted to be his wife.

“I have something to ask you,”

He stroked her arm, “Anything – you can ask me anything.”

“How would you feel about us giving this whole marriage thing a go?”

He sprang up onto his elbow and grinned. “Whoa, where did that come from?” he asked laughing.

“I don’t know, I was just thinking that maybe we could give being husband and wife a go – see how it goes for a while – check that we like it, and then… then maybe we might think about trying to make a little family.”

He kissed her on the forehead. “I like that idea very much,” he hesitated and Susan felt a knot in her stomach. “But we’ve still got a long way to go, Susan.”

She nodded. “I know. I do know that.”

“But it’s just the goal that we need. It’s hope.”

“Yes,” she agreed, “it’s hope.”

He reached out his hand and searched for hers. He loved the idea of making a family with her someday, but it was complicated.

"Tea?" she asked, swinging her legs out of bed.

"Please." He giggled. "Look at us being all rock 'n roll!"

"Yeah, well it's about as rock 'n roll as it's going to be from now on."

"I like that."

By the time she returned with the tea, Max was fast asleep. She put the tea down and crept back out of the room and downstairs to the lounge where her bag was still packed from her stay at Polly's. She searched down to the bottom of the bag and found the tiny box. She held it in her hand and allowed a few tears.

"What's that?"

The sound of Max's voice made her jump.

"I thought you were asleep."

He shrugged and looked at the box.

"I kept these all this time, it's the only thing I have of her." She carefully lifted the lid of the box. "The day I found out I was pregnant I bought these. I've carried them with me ever since. I don't think I can let them go."

Max enveloped her in his arms. "Then don't; don't let them go. It doesn't mean you're going to forget her, or replace her. They're part of you."

"Yeah, you're right – but they are part of me that needs closure. I think it's time to open up the attic and store a few things." She smiled weakly.

"That's a great idea, there are a few things I could do

with storing alongside yours. Now why don't I make us something to eat?"

Max cooked while Susan sat and watched him twirling her hair around the fingers.

The only thing spoiling this little moment of perfection was the thought of tomorrow's counseling appointment. Beth had a contact that she knew from her old university days and had managed to get her on her books; offering to help out with the fees. Secretly, Beth had reservations about the relationship between Susan and her son. Her mother's instinct fretted about the damage that had been done to Susan, and how that might in the end impact on her son; but he was a grown man, and a strong one at that. She had to accept his choices in life, and Susan deserved a chance at happiness. Susan had asked Beth to accompany her to the appointment, and she'd reluctantly agreed, telling her that she'd be happy to drive her there and pick her up, go for lunch afterwards, but she wouldn't come into the session – Susan had to start facing things by herself if there was ever a chance of her healing.

CHAPTER EIGHT

"Oh no, mister, you want to live here, you'll have to do you share of everything and I mean; cooking, cleaning, washing…" she counted the endless list of household chores on her fingers.

Max stood there with puppy eyes and his bottom lip sticking out like a child.

"I'm not joking, Max I'm not washing your sweaty socks!"

"Hey, my socks do not smell!" he said, throwing a sock over in her direction. She ducked and they giggled as he run over to her and bear-hugged her, sweeping her off her feet and twirling her around.

He took hold of her hands and leaned in to kiss her; she lent back and took in the sweet scent of his kiss; it was hypnotising. He moved her hands above her head and kissed her from the bottom of her neck to the top of her ear. He whispered seductively, "God I've missed you. I thought I had lost you forever. Promise me you won't ever do that again."

He let go of her hands and she placed them on either side of his face. "I promise." She sealed it with a kiss.

Susan stretched her arms out above her head and opened her eyes slowly. Max had left for work early, leaving Susan to get herself up and ready for her meeting with Dr. Holt. After waking herself up with a cup of coffee, she ran herself a relaxing bubble bath, after which she went to sit in the garden and wait for Beth to pick her up.

Dr. Holt greeted Susan with a friendly smile and a handshake before leading Susan over to the desk and instructing her to take a seat. She asked Susan a series and how she wanted to sessions to help her, making Susan feel more in control than she imagined she would.

"My advice, Susan is that for the moment you should keep a daily diary. Try to focus on one key factor we have discussed and then when you come in again we can look through it together. How does that sound to you?"

Susan flashed a smile and nodded.

Dr. Holt folded her arms across her chest. "Now, one more thing before you go, you briefly spoke about how you use alcohol to steady your emotions; I really feel you need to find something else to help you control your emotions. Do you have any hobbies? If you're interested, we have some wonderful social groups; you could join in the cooking group, or we have an art group – anything that will help you take back the control."

Susan thought for a moment before surprisingly opening up about her passion for art, explaining how her grandmother had taught her a selection of art techniques from a young age. Dr. Holt asked her to give it a try and see if it helped.

After finishing her afternoon coffee with Beth and shopping for supplies, she set up her canvas stand up in the sitting room. Before she knew it, she found herself passionately drawing the afternoon ocean setting. Pulling out the charcoal, she invoked herself into the paper, her fingers franticly rubbing over the image.

Max arrived home to Susan standing in front of the drawing, smiling.

"Hey baby, what have you been up to?" He walked up behind her, placing a kiss on her cheek. His eyes fell on the drawing. "Susan, did you do that?"

"Dr. Holt thought it might help, you know give myself a hobby."

"Susan that's amazing; I didn't know you could draw like that." The drawing took him by surprise, distracting him from what he set out to ask her.

The week past with more counseling sessions, dates with Max and watching box-sets curled up on the sofa. Every thing felt new and fresh, and Susan thought it time that they start to build their home together. Looking at the tired paint on the walls, she excitedly called Max from the kitchen and informed him that they were going to the DIY store. She had decided on a cheery yellow for the kitchen and a warm and cosy chocolate for the living room. Max convinced her to frame the drawing she had done and put it up in the living room.

"Susan, do we really need to all this stuff? We only came in for paint." Max frowned, loading his car with the new kitchen accessories.

"Of course I need to get all this; when a women decorates a room she need new accessories to go with the new color; it's the same with a new dress, you've got to buy new shoes and a handbag to match," Susan teased, as she leant out the car window.

Max shut the boot shaking his head. “I’ll never understand the woman’s mind!”

“Stop trying to,” she said giggling.

As Max unloaded all the new items from the car, Susan packed the old kitchen away into boxes. She had managed to convince Max that they needed a new kettle and toaster along with new cups, plates, pans and canisters. She dragged the dining table to the other end of the kitchen and began painting, concentrating around the door and window frame.

Max turned the music on and pulled a cold beer out the fridge. Leaning on the counter, her watched her, admiring the view of her working the brush up and down the wall. “My, my Miss Birch, you do look very sexy holding a brush in your hand.”

Susan didn’t answer, she took the brush and flicked it in his direction, spattering yellow droplets all over his crisp white t-shirt. “Now you’re covered in paint, you can grab the roller and help.”

Max walked over to the paint tray with a devilish look on his face. He picked the dripping roller up.

“Max! No!” she dropped the paintbrush into the tray and backed away from him.

Max drew closer. “But you don’t have any paint on you!” He backed her into the corner of the kitchen until she was unable to escape the roller.

“Max! Don’t you dare, I mean it!” She held up her hands to stop him but it was too late, he ran the roller all the way down the front of her shirt. “Max! I’m going to kill you!”

He turned and ran up the stairs, pulling his t-shirt off as he reached the top step. “Come and get me then.” He wore a seductive smile.

Susan stood on the bottom step slowly unbuttoning her shirt. She reached Max at the top step and pulled him to her until their lips met. Max lifted her up, curling her legs around his waist as he carried her into the bedroom.

“Come on Susan we are going to be late,” Max shouted up the stairs. Max was going to Jessop’s to play snooker and Susan had asked if she could come and watch.

“I’m coming now!” Dressed in black skinny jeans and a vest to with her curls falling over her shoulders. Max couldn’t resist letting out a low whistle.

“Wow! Do we really have to go out?” He wanted to take her back up stairs and make love to her.

“You promised you would take me to watch.”

“Are you sure you want to go?” he asked as he stroked her hair.

Susan pressed the keys into the palm of his hands. “Yes, I’m sure. We have plenty of time for that later, Max.”

“I’ll hold you to that”

*

Susan spent her afternoon watching Max in the garden as he cut the grass; she pretended to be reading but he knew she was checking him out. Just as he was about to hose her down with garden hose, Beth’s car pulled up outside.

“Hey, you two” she waved before grabbing a paper-bag full of patisseries from the bakery. “Beautiful day,” she said pushing her sunnies onto her head.

'It sure is!' Susan thought. 'About as perfect as it could get.'

Max packed away the lawnmower and Beth followed Susan into the kitchen.

"Sooo, how does it all feel?" Beth asked, sitting down at the table and unpacking the goodies. Susan turned from checking the chicken pie in the oven and flashed a look of confusion in Beth's direction.

"I mean how does it feel playing house?" Beth said smiling.

Susan laughed. "Let's just say we are settling in just fine."

"Good – you both look so happy. It's good to see."

As the three of them sat down to eat, Beth told Susan about her next appointment and how she felt confident enough to make the trip on her own, although it would still be nice to meet up after lunch. Beth smiled, taking it as a really positive sign that Susan was beginning to take control over things.

After tea, Beth and Max cleared the table as Susan headed to the wine rack with the thought of opening a bottle to drink in the garden. Max was behind her like a shot and whispered, "I'm not sure that is a good idea."

Susan fired him a look and muttered angrily, "Excuse me!" But she was angrier with herself than Max – he had a point but she didn't want to admit it.

"Why don't I make us some coffee instead?"

"I don't want coffee!" she replied with gritted teeth. "I want a glass of wine with your mother in the sunshine." Beth glanced in their direction and continued wiping up.

Susan wasn't finished, "I'm not going to go off the rails and drink the whole fucking bottle you know."

Max kept his voice lowered, "I know. I know. It's just that …"

With that Susan stormed off into the living room.

She could hear Beth and Max talking in the kitchen in muted tones and she felt a flush of embarrassment. Max deserved better.

Beth came in to thank Susan for lunch, and to say that Max was walking her home. She kissed Susan on the cheek before heading out of the door and leaving her alone. Susan headed upstairs for a shower and a nap. When she came back downstairs Max still wasn't back. She sent him a text asking what was taking him so long but she didn't't get a reply.

She sat on the sofa and watched the sea from the window. It was so peaceful; she lost herself in the horizon. The day faded and the house became dark. Still he wasn't home. She made herself a cup of tea, tried to read, thought about opening the bottle of wine, but didn't. In the end she headed upstairs. She woke in the morning to an empty bed; her nerves shot with the thought that maybe he wasn't coming back. She crept along the landing and saw that the door to the spare room was open. Max was tucked up under the covers, fast asleep.

She crept in to the room and climbed into the bed beside him, wrapping her hand around his. She felt his arms come around her waist and he opened his eyes and looked at her.

"I'm sorry," she whispered, giving him a small smile and leaning her head on his shoulder.

"I know."

"You're right. I know that you're right," she said.

He shook his head. "You're a grown up, you've got to make your own choices."

"I choose you."

He smiled and stroked her head.

"Good."

They kissed and before they could think, their hands and bodies took over. Their lovemaking was tinged with anger – which felt good in its own way.

The next morning, Max left for work without waking her to say goodbye and she knew that he was still mad with her. She sent him a text to say 'good morning' and went downstairs to make some breakfast. She had a few hours before her therapy session and she needed moral support. She phoned Polly.

As ever, Polly was full of wisdom and sense. She told her to relax, and that they were going through a period of adjustment, there were bound to be moments of tension. She told her to stop moping around and fix it – take charge. It was just the thing she needed to hear.

"Thanks, Polly – I've got a great idea."

They finished their conversation with arrangements to meet up for dinner in a couple of days. After finishing the call, she flipped through the photos on her phone and found one of the two of them on the beach together smiling.

She set off early to give herself time to stop off at the chemist to print out the photos. On the walk to the doctor's office, she passed a little shop and saw just what she was looking for, a lovely photo-frame. She went inside and asked if they had anymore, the women went to look in the back and came back carrying a box.

Pleased, Susan said, "I'll take the box please, how much?"

Confused the women answered, "Well, ah, let me see, thirty pounds please."

Susan handed her the money and checked her watch. She had just enough time to swing into the supermarket and grab something nice for dinner. She'd truly screwed up last night and she needed to make it up – big style.

It was her second visit to see Dr. Holt. She was also a GP and so as well as a lot to think about, she came out clutching a green prescription slip. She felt uneasy; she didn't know what to think about being prescribed medication. She wasn't depressed – she felt happier than she had in a long time.

The meetings with the counselor were going better than Susan had expected and they agreed that weekly ongoing meeting would be the best option. In their sessions, they would address each aspect of her life with a clear focus point, breaking it down so that it didn't seem so overwhelming. She felt good afterwards; it helped to know she wasn't been judged. They also decided Susan should keep a diary of each day and take it with her each week; it was intended to help her overcome the emotions she felt.

On the way to the car park was a small jewellery shop, which pulled her in like a magnet. Staring out from a little velvet cushion was *the* ring. "It's perfect," she said to to herself, smiling and feeling like a giddy schoolgirl. It was a simple white gold ring with two diamonds. "Almost perfect." She pushed the door open and jostled her bags in.

After discussing her idea with the jeweler, they arranged for her to pick it up in a couple of weeks.

At home, Susan put dinner on. Max would be home in an hour so she had plenty of time to get the rest of the surprise ready. Pulling the photos out, she then pulled out the six photo frames. She smiled with satisfaction. They were gorgeous, silver plated with rose-vines entwined around the frame. She set them all in a row on the table and picked which pictures to put in them. She found the one of the two of them at the beach pulling a silly face, and the one of them in Paris. A nice woman had taken it for them. She also found the one of her that Max had taken as a joke when she was asleep in bed. She put them all in the frames and put them out on the dresser in the living room, before heading upstairs to get changed. She slipped on the purple dress; the one that he couldn't wait to get her out of last time. She headed over to the mirror and let her curls drop over her shoulders before applying a bit of lipstick. "Ready!" she said, taking in a deep breath.

She heard Max came into the kitchen. "Something smells good," he called. He was waiting at the bottom of the stairs and gave her a small smile when he saw her.

"Do I have time for a quick shower before dinner?"

Susan looked at him hurt, he hadn't said anything about her dress or how much effort she had gone too. She nodded and carried on to the kitchen, watching him over her shoulder as he went upstairs. "Take charge!" she whispered, remembering Polly's words. She turned off the oven and followed him upstairs. Creeping into the bathroom, she let the dress slip to the floor before opening the shower door.

"What the hell are you doing?" Max asked whipping the water off his face. "You nearly gave me a fucking heart attack."

She stepped into the shower and wrapped her arms around him. "I just wanted to join you," she said as she kissed his back.

Max spun, wrapped his arms around her and kissed her head chastely. It wasn't the reaction she'd been hoping for – she'd kind of hoped to be ravished.

"Sweetie, do you mind if I take a shower on my own? I'm really tired. I'll be down in a minute."

He knew that he was pushing her away and being unkind, but his head was crammed full of thoughts; he loved her more than anything – but it wasn't easy. He wasn't sure he was strong enough to carry her, even though he desperately wanted to.

She climbed out of the shower, stepped over her dress and went to the bedroom to put on her sweat pants. She really couldn't understand why he was being so distant.

Max joined her in the living room. On seeing the photos he asked, "Where did all these come from?"

His question had an edge about it – it wasn't the glee she'd hoped for. She didn't reply but walked through the kitchen to the garden. She needed fresh air. Max stood alone in the living room staring at the pictures; each told its own story. He smiled at the one of them on the beach; it was the night she had run laughing. Then he saw the picture of her sleeping, he picked it up he carried it with him to the garden

"Can we talk?" he asked.

She'd been crying. Her beautiful, blue eyes were now all red and puffy – her cheeks rosy with the cold.

"Whatever you have to say, Max, just say it. I'm not playing games anymore and I'm tired."

Max held the picture up. "I love this picture of you. Want to know why?"

She shrugged.

"I took this the first night we slept together. You looked so peaceful, like an angel. I couldn't stop watching you. In that moment I knew I wanted to spend the rest of my life with you." He took hold of her face before continuing, "I love everything about you; your eyes, your smile. I love to twirl my fingers in your hair. I love every bit of your body. However, your mind scares me. When I found you drunk in the park I thought you were dead for fuck's sake, and then I get you home and you go for the bottle of wine… I just don't know what to do. Things are a bit of a mess." He let go of her face and ran his fingers through his hair.

"I understand," she muttered. Susan looked at him. Since he'd found her, he has been walking on eggshells; they couldn't live like this. She stood up and held out her hand. "But things are different. Can I show you something?"

Max nodded and she guided him into the house.

When they got in the living room, she took the photo out of his hand and put it back on the dresser then stood back. "I picked these photos for a reason. I know they all mean something to you. I didn't do this for me, I did it for you." She walked over to the window and crossed her arms taking in a deep breath.

"Max, I can't change anything that has happened – I

wish you hadn't found me like that – I wish we could just be normal, but we, I mean I'm not. I've got baggage and you know that. I'm trying to deal with it, but I can't do it alone. The bottle was a mistake. I kid myself that I can have a drink like a 'normal' person, and mostly I can, but often I take it to numb the pain – and maybe I have lost sight of the difference.

Max walked over and put his finger on her lips. "You don't have to explain."

"Max, I don't need you to save me. I've got to do that myself. But I would like your support – and that means just being here for me."

Max locked his arms around her. "That's all I want, to be here for you," he whispered. "Let's get out of here for a bit."

"I know the perfect place." Then she headed out of the door with Max behind her. The two walked hand in hand down to the beach and sat watching the sunset in silence.

This is where their magic came from; this was the place where nothing could touch them. Here they felt safe and Susan wished they could spend the rest of their life sat here, in this spot. After there was no more sun to set, Max stood up and held his hand out for Susan. They walked back to the house and ate dinner in candlelight before going to bed and holding each other.

The next couple of weeks felt like a dream. They woke up together, ate together and went to sleep together; she even turned up at the garage one day to take him out to dinner. Polly moved into Beth's and they got on like a house on fire; already becoming firm friends. Polly would be here for good she couldn't ask for anymore than that. Max had come home from his mother's with boxes of paperwork to do with the garage. She didn't have a clue were they were going to go; the house was three bedroom so maybe they could turn one into an office – better still the dining room.

Watching him moving in his work, made Susan feel content – it was a massive signal that he was staying for good. "Max," she shouted out to the car. "Come here a minute." He came in carrying a huge box. She opened the door to the dining room "What about using this as your office? I never use this room, it's just full of boxes that could go up in the loft."

Max looked into the room. "I think that would be perfect, we could start over the weekend. I'll take Monday and Tuesday off."

"That sounds great. Food?" she asked heading to the kitchen.

"Hmmm well there's nothing in here I can make a meal with, but you can," she laughed, shaking a box of eggs at him.

Max grabbed the box off her and pushed her out the way with his bottom. "Move aside, women, time for me to work my magic." Susan slapped his rear on her walk to the living room, shouting after her, "Work away, MAN!"

CHAPTER NINE

Susan woke, checked the clock and shot out of bed. Max hadn't woken her this morning and she had a million things to do today before Polly and Beth came for a BBQ that evening. She quickly showered, dressed and rushed downstairs, before heading off to the garage.

When she arrived, Max was in the office. She walked through, offering a greeting to the other guys that worked there. Max was on the phone and so she waited for him to finish. "Can I have some car keys, I need to run a few errands?" she stood, holding her hand out for the keys.

Max stretched over and dropped them into her hand." Are you picking me up when you're done?" he asked, pulling her in for a kiss.

Susan unravelled from his grip. "Yeah, sure, I'll come when I'm finished. Okay, see you later." She climbed into the car and drove into town.

When she arrived at the jewellery shop, the jeweller already had the ring ready and boxed, waiting for her under the counter. Taking a quick look, she smiled, paid and left for the supermarket.

Susan had it all planned. They would have a lovely BBQ to officially celebrate Polly's arrival in town, and then she would ask Max to marry her. She knew that some people would say she was rushing it – her counselor for one – but they had a lifetime of love to make up for, and she had been away from him for too long.

She parked outside the garage, waiting for him to lock

up, pipping the horn to tell him to hurry up. She couldn't stop herself checking him out – there was something about the way he looked when he was all greased up that really got her going. She fantasised about having him here and now, over the bonnet of the car. 'He could have anyone he wants,' she thought, 'especially looking the way he does right now – but he chose me.'

"What are you looking at?" His voice snapped her out of her daydream.

Licking her lips, she gave him a devilish look. "Oh, I was just admiring the view." He laughed and flopped into the passenger seat.

*

"I just have to do something before we start getting ready." She kissed him hard.

"What?" he asked as he removed his coat and shoes.

Susan looked at him longingly. "I need to get you up the stairs right now – because if I don't get you into bed, I'm going to explode."

Max stood for a moment in the hallway gob-smacked, before rushing up the stairs, shedding his clothes as he went. She was on the bed waiting for him in nothing but her lacy slip. He smiled, pulled off his remaining clothes and climbed up the bed towards her, grinning. "What has got into you?" he whispered in her ear.

Before he knew it, he was on his back and she was on top of him, kissing his chest. Her hands moving over his body. He was so ready for her, but she made him wait – taking control. Max was in sweet heaven with every move she took. She sat up and flung her hair behind her, moving with an urgent rhythm, racing each other to climax. His shoulders ached from her grip. They cried out together and after a moment of ecstasy, flopped, gasping for breath.

"You, Miss Birch are a very bad influence, do you know that?" Max laughed, stoking her hair.

Susan giggled. "Don't tell me you didn't enjoy that." Her fingers curled around his chest hair and she smiled smugly.

Max kissed her forehead and replied. "Well don't get me wrong, I enjoyed that; a lot. It was just unexpected, that's all, and we have guests arriving soon." He looked at his watch and giggled, "Like in fifteen minutes!"

"Shit!" She ran around the bedroom finding something suitable to wear whilst Max jumped into the shower. She tied her hair up in a ponytail, put some makeup on before pulling her dress on, and went downstairs to find her shoes. Max came down ten minutes later looking smoking hot. Her heart beat faster the closer he got to her. What the hell was up with her? She wanted him more and more the last few days; her appetite was almost insatiable.

She shook herself out of it; Beth and Polly were due any minute.

She headed out to the garden with a bottle of Becks Blue, (Max had given up alcohol in show of support) and handed it to him. The sun was shining. Life couldn't be any more perfect. The doorbell rang and she skipped through the house, opening it to face a big bouquet of flowers and Polly and Beth juggling bowls of salad and summer pudding. Susan giggled, kissing and hugging them both chaotically. This is what had been missing in her life all this time. The afternoon slid into evening and was full of laughter, chat and good food.

Susan's face almost hurt from smiling. Butterflies danced in her tummy. In a short while she would be asking the man she loved to marry her. It would be an endless dream coming true.

Their relationship had grown so fast, she hoped inside that one day soon they would be able to call themselves a complete family. Although she'd made a conscious decision not to think about the whole baby thing, it didn't work like that. The sight of a pram in the park, a little one in a supermarket trolley, children playing on the beach, all caused her to stop and long for the day that she was no longer an outsider.

Max stood up to go in and make some more punch. Beth echoed him, gathering up an armful of dirty crockery. When they'd left, Polly turned to Susan and asked,

"Are you okay honey? You don't look so bright." She placed her hand on Susan forehead.

"I'm fine! Just feeling a little nervous, that's all."

Susan had shared her surprise proposal plans with Polly earlier that day. She hadn't come away with the impression that Polly was overjoyed about the idea. She'd said the 'right' things, but there had been a slight hesitation that Susan knew only too well as being one of concern.

Polly took a deep breath and dropped her voice to almost a whisper. "Don't bite my head of Susan, but I have to ask you something – and it's because I care."

Susan sighed heavily – she'd guessed as much. "Polly, will you just spit it out please."

"Okay." Polly shifted in her seat. "Are you sure about

all of this? It's just that it's all happening so fast; I mean this thing with Max; marriage, setting up home… a baby? Are you really ready for all of this? I just don't want to see you rush in and get hurt – maybe you need more time." She shrugged and put her hand on Susan's knee. "What did your counselor say about it?"

Susan stood up, gathering up the remaining dishes. "And you decide to say all this *now*? Of course, I'm sure! Do you really think I'd go through with it if I wasn't ready?"

Polly looked down at the floor and twitched. "Babe, I'm sorry but a part of me thinks you would. It was only a month or so ago that you were convinced you couldn't have children – and now you're already talking about being a family. What if it doesn't all happen smoothly? What if you have to face disappointments? I just don't want to see you hurt if it doesn't go your way."

Shock washed over Susan's face. "I can't believe what you're saying. I love Max; he means the world to me. I know we haven't been together long but I've known him all of my life. Please just have some faith in me."

Polly twiddled with the stem of her glass and said softly, "That's not always easy, Susan. Sometimes your behaviour is quite self-destructive. I think you're searching for someone to rescue you – and Max is an easy option."

Susan's eyes widened with hurt.

"He's a really good man, Susan – he'll make a wonderful husband, but he's not your savior – that's up to you. This whole baby thing – you need to see the bigger picture. What happens if in a year or two you're still trying for a baby? What happens if it never happens – will Max be enough for you? Will you end up hurting him?"

Susan looked over to the kitchen window and watched Max with his mum. As much as what Polly had said hurt her, she knew that Polly loved her. It was Polly's brutal honesty that had pulled her through the dark days.

"I understand your worry, but when I'm with him I see more clearly than I have before. He has shown me that there is hope for anything. Do you remember what I was like when you found me?" Polly nodded. "Max proved to me that I have nothing to be frightened of – not with him around. He won't let me down. He's strong and he's loyal."

Polly had never seen Susan smile like the way she did when Max was around; it was magical to watch. She could almost feel the connection they shared together. There was no doubting their love. Polly smiled at Susan. "I suppose I need to let you start making your own choices."

Susan wrapped her arms around Polly. I will always need you but I don't need you to worry. You got me back on my feet and into the world. I will always be grateful for that. I will always love you for that."

Polly knew it was time she let Susan go – it was just hard; she was like a sister. Max and Beth returned with a big jug of punch, some more alcohol free beers in an ice bucket and Beth's infamous summer pudding.

"What are you two up to?" Max asked grinning.

Polly stood up and announced that she was visiting the loo. As she passed Max she muttered, "Promise me you will look after her, Max?"

Max's face twisted in bemused confusion.

"What did she say to you?" Susan asked.

Max kissed her forehead. "Oh nothing much." He

shrugged.

"Are you two alright – Polly seems a little..."

Susan smiled reassuringly, "No, she's alright – just women's talk; emotions running high, that type of talk."

Max laughed. "Ah, *that* kind of talk."

Beth sat down and poured a drink. "Talking of emotions being high; I wondered if you would like to meet some more of the family. My sister and her children, Max's cousins are planning a visit – it would be nice for you to get to know them."

Susan smiled at her. "That sounds perfect, thank you, Beth. Actually talking of family, I've been thinking I need to make a visit of my own, would you mind going to visit my family's graves with me tomorrow; I don't want to go alone."

"Of course, sweetheart. I'd be honored."

They finished the rest of the punch, demolished the summer pudding and chatted until the air turned chilly, taking it as their cue to go. After lots of hugs and kisses, Max and Susan were left alone.

"Fancy a walk?" Susan asked.

"Yeah, sure, that would be nice."

Susan had planned everything carefully, packing a wicker picnic basket earlier with all the essential proposal equipment; candles, blanket, bottle of Perrier water and a couple of champagne glasses – as well as the little velvet box tucked in the bottom. As Susan gathered up her shawl and the basket, Max eyed it with curiosity but didn't say anything. It was a day full of surprises.

They headed down to the beach, taking their shoes off to feel the still warm sand between their toes. When Susan was happy with the spot, she put down the basket, spread out the blanket and set up the space.

"This all looks very suspicious – what are you up to, Susan?" he asked, wrapping his arms around her.

Susan flopped onto the blanket and giggled. "Can't I be romantic?" She patted the spot next to her.

Max sat down and took his glass of water, joking, "Champagne tastes better!"

"Yeah, too right – I'm going to miss Champagne."

"It's a small price to pay."

They sat quietly looking out to sea. The moon was full and shed a silvery light.

She moved to sit between his legs, relishing the security. "I know how I feel now."

"What do you mean babe?" he asked in her ear, his lips brushing over her hair.

"I mean, I know what my heart wants. All this time I knew something was missing in my life, it wasn't kids and it wasn't family past or future." She turned taking a deep breath. "The missing piece was you, it always was. You have given me life."

"Oh, baby." Max wrapped his arms around her. "I love you."

"I love you too."

Their conversation drifted into quiet. Susan was building up to ask her question.

"I love this place." Susan's voice was soft.

Max turned to look at her. "Me too"

"I would love to get married here. It would be perfect, don't you think?" she smiled, waiting for his response.

"Yeah, it would be." Max wrapped his arms around her.

Susan turned around, kneeling in front of him. “Let’s do it then. Let’s get married here.”

Max let out a laugh. “Right now? I don’t think that would count do you?”

When Max looked down she was holding a white gold ring in front of him.

“Are you serious?” he said, smiling.

Susan passed him the ring and laughed. “Yes, of course I’m serious. I want to spend the rest of my life with you, and I don’t want to wait or slowdown, I just want you now and forever.”

“Me too. Of course I’ll marry you.” He took the ring from her. What does it say?

She looked at him in the moonlight. “*In this place, we are complete.*”

He knew exactly what that meant. “Come here,” he said, placing the ring on his left ring finger.

Susan jumped up and threw her arms around him.” I can’t believe it. It’s going to be perfect.” She kissed him and tears of happiness trickled down her cheeks.

*

Susan woke and the space next to her was empty and cold. It was still dark outside. She Jumped out the bed and started to look for him. She checked everywhere but couldn’t find him – not even outside: there was no sign of him. She picked up her phone but the battery was dead. She went to the beach, but he was not there. When she returned to the house, all the lights were off. Where was he? She checked every room again but this time, when she checked the office none of his stuff was there. It was just filled with boxes. She ran upstairs frantically shouting out for him. She ran into the bedroom and opened the drawers. Nothing. Fear washed over her.

Her eyes flew open to see Max lying beside her, fast asleep. Heat washed over her. She lifted herself out of the bed and walked into the bathroom. She felt light headed and a crippling pain shot across her stomach just before she threw up. Trying not to wake Max up, she cleaned herself up, got a glass of water and curled back up into bed wrapping herself around him.

Next morning, Susan sat waiting for Beth to pick her up. Nerves washed over her; she had never been to the graves before and now she had a whirlwind of emotions inside her, she began to feel sick. Just then the car pulled up outside the house.

The ride was quiet; neither said much on the way there. When they arrived at the cemetery, Beth put her arm around Susan. “Are you okay?”

Susan took a breath and nodded. She was as ready as she would ever be. All three graves were in a row together. Kneeling down between her mum and dad’s, tears ran down her face. She had been so young when they had died; she hadn’t really understood what their death meant; the years of loss, and emptiness. Beth handed her two of the three bunches of flowers. She turned to her grandmother’s grave and laid the bunch of roses. Her grandmother had been an angel, and it was cruel that God had called her home too soon.

After twenty minutes of sitting, she cleared her throat

and whispered, "Goodbye Mum, goodbye Dad." Although Susan tried to control the sobs, they broke free. Beth stood back – grief needed release.

When Susan had managed to recover herself, Beth stepped forward with a single rose. "You forgot one," she said.

Susan turned and looked at her confused. "Beth, what do you mean?"

Beth took her hand. "I think you know. Lay the flower with your folks and say your peace; let them take her with them. She squeezed Susan's hand and walked to the car.

Susan stood holding the rose, not minding the thorns. Beth was right, it was time to say her peace. She bent down in the empty space between her parents and her grandmother, kissed the rose and placed it down between them. "I think about you everyday, I always have. You never got to know what it felt like to be loved, but you are. In my heart you are always loved. Goodbye, sweetheart, I will never forget you." Susan stood up and blew a kiss before rejoining Beth at the car.

She felt overwhelmed with emotions, but good emotions; she felt happy that she finally got to say goodbye to them all and she had a place she could come to whenever she needed to check in. Smiling, she climbed in the car with Beth. "Thank you, you've no idea what that meant to me."

Beth smiled. "I think I do."

CHAPTER TEN

Susan climbed out of bed to the smell of breakfast cooking. She felt her stomach twist and her head pounded; she recalled with annoyance that her period was due; always a chore. She groaned remembering that she also had counseling session, which was okay in itself, but they always left her feeling a little edgy, and in need of a large glass of wine. Max was still very much on the 'no drinking' thing, which she knew was for the best, but really took a shine off things.

She was confused why Max hadn't left for work; he hadn't mentioned taking leave. When she got to the kitchen door, he was placing eggs onto a plate. "Hey, sleepy head, I tried waking you but…" He shrugged and smiled at her as she sat down.

She took a sip of her coffee. It tasted odd, as if it had gone stale. "Why are you not at work yet?" she said

He walked to the dining room door and opened it. "We were going to sort through these boxes, remember?" The pile of ten or so boxes had been piled up to make space for Max's paperwork and office stuff but they needed to be sorted before putting them in the attic.

"Ah, yeah, I forgot all about that." Susan's memory had been playing tricks on her the last couple of days, she kept forgetting little things and she put it down to the emotional roller coaster she was riding. "But I've got my session this morning." Looking at the clock, she realised that meant it was in less than an hour.

"It's okay, while you're out I'll drag the boxes into the living room. What's in them, anyway?" Max quizzed.

Susan was tucking into her eggs. She was starving and didn't really want to be bothered with a full on conversation. She said between mouthfuls, "They were left when my grandmother died. They got put into storage by the estate agent and then moved back when I came back. I think he must have had a sweet spot for Gran."

Finishing her breakfast, she ran upstairs to get ready when Max came into the bedroom. He looked at his watch and raised an eyebrow whilst flashing a sexy little smile.

"No you don't," she laughed, "Get out, I'm already running late and you're distracting me."

Max crossed his arms and leaned in the doorway, checking her out. "I have no idea what you're talking about, but you do look very yummy in that."

Susan threw a cushion at him and chased him out of the room. It felt good to be so wanted.

Susan parked the car and walked to the doctor's with her notebook tucked under her arm. The session revolved around her family and to her surprise, it went really well. The visit to the cemetery with Beth had helped a lot. She had written a lot of her feelings down in the book that day and things started to make sense. Dr. Holt agreed that she had opened up a lot not just in the book but also to her.

Dr. Holt told her that she was pleased with how the session had gone and that she should focus on one obstacle at a time. It was important to keep writing everything down for them to review. Dr. Holt wanted to spend next session exploring Susan's possible dependency on Max. The journal revealed intense around Max. She had written down about her 'craving him more' over the last couple of weeks and Dr. Holt explained that it could be side effects from the medication or it could be an increased sense of needing reassurance and security. Susan didn't tell Dr. Holt that she hadn't taken her anti-depressant medication in over a month; she'd abandoned it along with her contraceptive pill, which was probably why she was suffering such hideous PMT.

By the time Susan arrived home, Max had pulled all the boxes out from the office and was sat on the floor with a bottle of champagne and two glasses.

She eyed him cautiously.

"I thought we could make an afternoon of it?" he said grinning.

Susan smiled and sat down next to him. "I thought drink wasn't allowed."

Max opened the bottle and poured her a glass. "Well I've been thinking that we haven't really celebrated our engagement, have we?" He kissed her and passed her the glass. "I've got to trust you." He'd been thinking whilst she'd been out; doing his own bit of talk-therapy and he came to understand that he couldn't wrap her up in bubble wrap, as much as he wanted to. They needed to try and lead a normal life.

They emptied the first two boxes, which were just filled with old bills and books, putting most of the contents into a heavy-duty black bin liner. They stacked the books in a pile to the side of them.

Max pulled the next box over and opened it. They found

photos of Susan as a baby with her parents, photos of her with her grandmother and photos of her playing with Max in the garden.

"We should get some of these framed up."

"Yeah, I'd like that," Susan said sadly. "It would be nice to rebuild my history."

Max pulled an envelope from the bottom of the box. "I think this is for you." Passing it to her, she noted her name on the front. She pulled herself back up onto the sofa and took a deep breath. Inside was a small folded piece of paper.

My dear Susan,

Forgive the sentimentality of an old lady, but I'm not as young as I used to be and I worry about the future; I worry about never seeing you graduate or marry, or have children. Although I have plans on being there for all of these things, I'm writing this as a bit of an insurance policy!

I hope I will be with you the day you marry your love, but if I am not, I want you to know two things; when you find him, don't ever let him go, no matter what happens. If he is your true love, it won't matter what happens, he will still love you.

Secondly, keep your mum and dad close to your heart; it's where they belong. They loved you more than you can ever know. Be strong, be kind, and be good.

I will always be with you

Grandma x

The envelope slipped from her lap, weighted down by

something inside. She picked it up and tipped it out. In the bottom of the envelope were two gold wedding bands, her parent's. She folded the letter and put it away and then sat and stared at the rings in the palm of her hand. Max put his hand on her knee and offered her a sympathetic smile. He had endured the pain of losing his father; he couldn't imagine what it must have been like to lose both parents.

The letter had distressed her, making her sad and happy at the same time. She rushed to the bathroom just in time to throw up down the toilet.

Max passed her a glass of water. "Are you okay, babe?"

Taking a sip of her water she didn't know how she felt. "I think so." She brushed her hair out of her face. "I think it's just the shock." She went back downstairs and packed everything away.

"Can you just put the rest in the loft as they are? I'm not ready to do the rest yet."

"Sure thing, babe."

She didn't know what to do about the rings; she didn't really have any memories about her parents but they were still her parents. They didn't want to leave her, it wasn't their fault – and yet, somehow it felt like it was. As Max lifted the boxes, Susan watched. The last one, slipped from his hands and the contents scattered across the floor. It was some of Susan's baby clothes and toys.

He held up a tiny, yellow summer dress. "I cannot imagine you in this," he said, trying to lighten her mood.

Susan laughed, taking hold of the dress. All the time she grew up in London she had had nothing from her childhood.

Max picked up the scattered things and put them back

in the box. "Loft for these too?"

Susan nodded, but held onto the yellow dress like a comforter.

That night, Susan struggled getting to sleep. Her head was full with thoughts of the rings, the letter and everything else they had found in the boxes. When she finally drifted off to sleep, her dreams gave her the answer. For the first time, she dreamt of her parents playing in the garden with her, laughing and joking. Susan giggled until it hurt as her dad span her around in his arms. She did have happy memories, she had just buried them, like treasure, to keep them safe.

When she woke, Max had already left for work. Later that morning he sent her a text telling her that he'd be late. Sickness washed over her and she felt crippling pain in her stomach. She headed off to bed with a book, drifting off to sleep. She woke several time to throw up and tracked back what she'd eaten, certain that the prawn sandwich she'd had for lunch yesterday had been dodgy.

"Hey, sleepy head. Are you feeling any better?"

She opened her eyes to Max leaning over her with a glass of water. Taking a sip, she threw the glass back at him and ran in the bathroom to throw up once more.

He helped her back to the bed and tucked her in under the cover before heading down stairs.

She opened he eyes to darkness. She flicked on the light and headed to the bathroom. There was nothing left for her to puke up, but that didn't stop the feeling of nausea. She looked in the bathroom mirror at her reflection; she looked a mess. Her eyes had big dark rings under them and her face was pale.

Susan slept until late in the afternoon, waking occasionally to the sound of Max opening the door to check on her. When she eventually got out of the bed, her legs wobbled a little. She managed to get herself to the bathroom before she threw up all over the toilet bowl.

"Susan?" Max flung the door open. "Hey it's okay, come on, lets get you back to bed."

"Max, its okay, I just need some air." Susan stared to walk down the stairs.

"I really wish you would rest baby." Max took her arm to steady her, leading her to the kitchen table. "Maybe try having something to eat that might make you feel better."

Susan smiled at him from across the table. "Yeah, just a slice of toast though."

After finishing her toast, she began to feel a little more normal and Max poured her a coffee. "Baby I got you an appointment with the doctor, today"

"What? Max, no, I feel fine now." She took a sip of her coffee.

"No buts, Susan, we leave in twenty minutes." He gave her a kiss on the forehead and left to go and get dressed.

As the car pulled up outside the doctors butterflies fluttered in Susan's stomach, her nerves took over. Max had to be worrying over nothing she just had a stomach bug that's all.

The surgery was busy and they had to wait for nearly an hour. It was made worse by the heating being on full blast. At last they were called in. After a quick discussion about her symptoms, the doctor examined her.

"Well let's just have a little feel of your tummy and then I'll take your temperature and blood pressure, okay?"

Susan nodded as she climbed on the bed and pulled her top up over her belly, his hands felt cold on her skin and she flinched at his touch. He worked his hand over her stomach pushing and prodding. As she sat up on the bed her checked her blood pressure mumbling the numbers before checking her temperature.

"Okay, Susan, I need you to give me a urine sample. You can use the toilet next door and just come straight back in here after."

She returned five minutes later looking flustered.

"Is there any chance that you could be pregnant, Susan?" the doctor asked.

Susan looked at Max and blushed. "I don't think so… I mean, I don't think I can get pregnant.

Max reached out for her. They both sat in silence as the doctor did the test and returned to click some notes into the computer. He turned to them and smiled,

"Now then, Susan, your blood pressure is a little on the high side but your temperature is fine, so that's a good thing. As for the sickness, that's to be expected in your condition."

Max cut the doctor off, "What condition?"

"He's saying I'm pregnant!" Susan said, not daring to believe it.

The doctor continued with business, "I'll book you an appointment at the hospital for your first scan and they'll be able to tell you your due date and such. Going from the dates you've given me, you're probably a good couple of months on."

With everything that had been going on she had lost track. Max squeezed at her hand to get her attention, giving her a wink. All she could think about was the regrettable night she had slept with the guy from the bar and ended up off her face in the park.

All the way home, she tried to silently calculate the weeks, her cycle and the possibilities of getting pregnant. Every time she got close to working it out, it slid messily into the night she had cheated on Max. *'That would be my luck,'* she thought. *'Every chance of happiness is cursed.'*

She texted Polly and asked her to meet her at the house. She signed it off with 'URGENT!!!!'

As the car pulled up, Polly was already waiting. When Max raised an eyebrow, Susan said, "It's a big thing, Max – a really big thing. I just need to process it with Polly. I don't want to spoil anything about this by unloading on you; we'll talk and celebrate later."

"Okay," he said, clearly not happy that their time was being gatecrashed. Polly greeted Max with a smile and he grunted, heading in.

"We're going for a walk, back in an hour," Susan said.

"What's the matter?" Polly asked wrapping her arms around Susan.

"I need to talk to you… now" Susan's response came out firm as she headed in the direction of the beach.

"What am I going to do?" Susan sobbed, barely able to get her words out.

Polly held her hand. "What did the doctor say?"

"Oh, Polly, I'm pregnant." She fell into uncontrollable

crying.

"Hey! Hey, ssshhhh! It's going to be okay; this is good news: amazing news! It's what you have been hoping for."

Polly tried to comfort her but nothing could make any of this okay. "I don't think you understand, I can't be sure that the baby is Max's. What if he leaves me?"

"What do you mean, 'you can't be sure'?"

Susan couldn't look Polly in the eye. "You know you said that sometimes my behavior was self-destructive – well you we're right. I do stupid things – all the time; things I regret. Things that end up hurting me."

"What are you on about?"

"I did something really stupid, this time."

"Look, Susan, I can't help you if you don't tell me."

"I slept with someone else – when I left Winchelsea, and came back to yours for those few weeks."

"What! When?"

"She waved he hand dismissively. "None of it really matters – didn't matter."

"Why did you do that, Susan?"

She shrugged, "I don't know. I was in a bar and this guy took the lead and I followed. I'd been drowning my sorrows – searching for the answer at the bottom of a bottle in my usual style."

Polly's hand rose to her mouth. "Oh, Susan! No, please, tell me this isn't true."

Susan shook her head.

"Does Max know?"

She shook her head, "I don't think so."

"Are you going to tell him?"

Susan burst into tears once more. Polly grabbed her

hands and pulled her closer. "It's going to be okay honey, whatever happens he isn't going to go anywhere. He loves you. He'll understand."

Letting her hands drop, Susan let out a big breath. "It's not the point, it wasn't meant to happen like this."

"Ssh, now you listen to me, he loves you, we love you, and nothing bad is going to happen! This is fantastic news. You are going to be the best mum in the world, and Max will be the best dad a child could want for."

Susan wiped her tears away. "You're right. It's just I can't believe this has happened so soon. I mean it's real, you know. I'm not sure I'm ready. What if something goes wrong?"

"Then we'll deal with it," Polly said. "Come on, Max needs some time with you – it's a big deal for him too." Polly took her by the hand and led her back to the house, stopping next to her car. "And, Susan, if you want my advice – don't tell Max about your concerns, not at the minute – not until you're certain. If you're wrong…" she shrugged and shot her a warning glance.

Susan knew Polly was right but it felt so wrong not sharing this with Max.

As soon as Polly left, Susan headed to the living room, curled herself into a ball on the sofa and closed her eyes. Her head thrashed over the day's events; a baby, how could it be? She placed her hand over the growing baby inside her. Max came in with a cup of hot chocolate and sat down on the floor by her side.

"Are you okay, baby?" Max's question was cautious.

"I think so... How are you?"

Max put his hand out and placed it on her stomach, smiling. “I’m ecstatic – you’re growing a baby... I... I mean, *we* are going to have a baby. I want to run and shout it down the streets.” He kissed her forehead. “But you don’t seem happy?”

“What happens if…?”

Max placed a finger on her lips and then kissed her passionately, leaving her hungry for more.

He sat quietly playing with the ring on his finger. “I promised you I’d never leave you. It doesn’t matter if the baby isn’t… “

Susan shot him a look. Her head spun. He seemed to know her concern – but how could he? Hesitantly she asked, “What do you mean, ‘if the baby isn’t?’ Are you suggesting that…?”

Max looked at her, pleading with her to abandon the conversation. Stupidly he had opened his mouth and now he knew he was risking everything – he really hadn’t meant to read her journal. He’d tried to ignore it lying on the bed. He’d walked past it twice before finally sneaking a look. He’d been hurt that she’d turned to Polly. It had seemed that between Polly and the damned counselor, everybody knew about her thoughts and feelings except for him.

Suddenly the understanding of what he must have done, hit her. Slowly, disbelieving the betrayal she said, “Oh, my God, you’ve read my journal! You know about what happened when I was staying at Polly’s. You’ve got the same doubts that I have! How could you? I trusted you, Max.”

He snorted and inhaled deeply. “That’s kind of rich!”

“What the fuck does that mean?”

“Well, if we’re talking trust here.”

Susan fell silent. Yes he’d betrayed her privacy – but his betrayal paled in significance next to hers. Max returned his hand to her stomach,

“It doesn’t matter. It really doesn’t. We’ve both been stupid. I don’t care whose DNA the baby has, we will be its mum and dad – you and me.”

Susan stared deep into Max’s eyes. For a moment, everything that they had been through in such a small space of time; all the pain she put him though had started to take its toll on him. His bright blue eyes no longer sparkled at the sight of her and the smile on his face rarely made an appearance recently. He looked tired and drained; so different to the man on the beach the first time they met. It filled her with sadness to look at what she’d caused. ‘I’ve done that to him,’ she thought.

“Max, have I told you you’re amazing, I love you so much,” she whispered softly snuggling into his shoulder.

“Let’s go to bed. I want to make love to you – I want to make this baby ours.”

Chapter 11

The moonlight glared through the window and Susan woke to an empty bed. Only this time, she wasn't dreaming. Standing up, she wandered across the landing to the spare room. Max lay on top of the bed, his fingers entwined across his head, almost as though he had fallen asleep while deep in thought. Careful not to step on the creaky floorboard, she crept over to his side and pulled the cover over him before leaning down and giving him a soft kiss on his forehead. She crept back to bed, pulling the door shut behind her.

Loneliness gripped her. So many questions ran through her mind. They'd only just begun to work through everything and now this… How could this happen?

Max had said everything was okay between them and that nothing mattered but it wasn't true; if it was true, he would be laying next to her now, not in the other bedroom alone. Would he stay? Could he love the tiny miracle growing inside her? If only she had been stronger when she had gone back to Polly's.

The faint sound of the alarm sprung Max's eyes open. Hitting the snooze button, he crept across the landing. His eyes shot to the bedroom door. It was closed. She had woken in the night, which meant she knew that he hadn't stayed by her side. He so badly wanted to crawl into bed next to her, to feel her body in his arms and make love to her… but something niggled him – and he was cross with himself that it did. Shaking his head, he opened the bathroom door. The image of a coward replaced his reflection in the mirror. All he could see was shame. She needed him now more than ever. The reflection made him angry. The reality of another man screwing her – making a baby with her, made his skin crawl. He'd lied to her when he had told her everything would be okay; it ate away at him from the moment he had read the words on the page. It didn't matter that she'd written all about the regret and shame – it had still happened, and now there was a lasting reminder of it – one that he'd have to face everyday. He had no one to share this with – he knew his mother would think that this had been a car-crash waiting to happen. She was very fond of Susan, but a mother is always going to protect her cub.

He slowly crept from the bathroom into her bedroom, holding his breath with every step he took. When he reached the bed he could tell she'd been crying, her beautiful eyes were red and puffy, the locks of her hair were tangled and twisted. He'd made her feel alone. He bent over and kissed her on the cheek before leaving the room.

For five days they lived different lives. They slept in different rooms (he using the excuse of wanting to give her proper rest) he worked late (blaming staff shortages) so that Susan was already in bed when he got home, and when they were in each other's company the same taboo conversations made them silent. Polly had kept her distance, which made Susan's feelings of isolation even worse.

But today, neither of them had work to do, the garage was closed nor there was no other reason to leave the house. Sunday was their lazy day. When she woke and went downstairs, she could hear the sound of cups and plates being arranged on the table and the smell of eggs and bacon filling the room. Max stood with his back to her; he was cooking whilst singing along to the radio. Watching him stood in nothing but his sweatpants sent a tingle down her spine. Edging herself over to him, she wrapped her arms around him and gave him a simple good morning.

Max jumped before spinning around and putting his arms around her neck. “Good morning to you too. I was going to bring this up to you.”

His display of affection took her off guard her for a moment. “Oh, sorry.” She tucked her hands up into her sleeves and sat at the table.

“I invited Mum and Polly to dinner, is that okay with you?” He smiled, passing her the plate breakfast.

No, it wasn’t alright with her; she didn’t want them here today. Today, she wanted it to be just the two of them. They needed to work on their relationship – they had some serious mending to do. “Max, what’s going on? she asked pushing the plate away. “I’m sorry, Max, but it’s not okay, I don’t want them here today; I wanted to spend the day with you – on our own.”

Max stood by the cooker, he couldn’t think of what to say, in the end he muttered, “I just thought you might like to see them, that was all. Mum’s really excited about the news and just wants to share it with us.”

“We need time, Max. We haven’t spoken, not properly, since the doctors. You’ve avoided me everyday since. Why, Max?” She lost her grip on the cup of coffee and it flew across the table, spilling everywhere. Max rushed to get the cloth, but she pulled it out his hand. “I’ll do it!” she snarled. She cleaned it up and then stormed off to the front room.

She turned on the TV and flicked through the channels pretending to be interested. His shadow loomed in the doorway, his arms crossed over his chest.

“I’m sorry, baby.” His head bent in shame. “I don’t know what to say. I’m sorry.” He walked over to the sofa and sat beside her.

“I can’t do this, Max, I can’t pretend like everything is okay; the working late, sleeping in the other room, I can’t do any of it. You’re either with me or not – just don’t pretend.”

“I know I can’t, Susan. I can’t pretend anymore. I can’t sleep another night without you. I can’t walk in this house and not be greeted with your smile.” He sighed, rubbing his head in his hands.

“Then don’t shut me out. I know none of this is how we planned but I can’t do it without you.”

“I’ll ring mum and tell her not to come.”

She looked at him and smiled. Relieved to have some time together.

“Tell me what your thinking?”

“I’m thinking you’re holding back on me, and not telling me how you really feel.”

Max paused for a moment unsure how to respond. “Susan I'm not hiding how I really feel, it’s just… it’s just, I don’t know how I feel. It’s a big thing to get my head around. You know I love you. Right?”

Susan gave a small smile, curling her feet up on the sofa. She nodded, “Yeah, so what’s the plan for today then?"

Max took hold of her hand, pulling her to her feet. He placed his hands on her waist. "I say that we get out of here for the day; what do you think?"

Just then his phone went off. Instinctively he pulled it out to check who the call was from. He grimaced and smiled apologetically. "Sorry, baby but I have to take this. It's Jake." He stepped into the hallway and took the call.

Susan went upstairs to get dressed. On the way down she pulled the dirty laundry from the basket and scooped it up in her arms heading back down the stairs. Max was waiting for her.

"I'm really sorry, baby; I've got to go into the garage. Shit timing, I know! If I could get one of the other boys, but they're all out and there's been a..."

Susan stood smiling but she wasn't happy – she wasn't even okay. "Of course you've got to go do what you have to."

In an instant he was off up the stairs to get ready, leaving Susan wanting, craving him, they hadn't made love in over a week.

Susan filled her lonely time cleaning the house and preparing dinner for when Max arrived home. When the clock reached 7:00pm she picked up the phone and sent him a text asking where he was. Giving up waiting for a reply, she ran herself a bath and went off to bed.

The faint touch of lips on her cheek woke her late in the night. Opening her eyes to the sight of Max made her smile, despite how angry she'd been at him earlier. She snuggled into him. She let her fingers run over his thigh. She loved everything about him. Not only had she cheated on him, but she'd stamped on his heart in the process. Forgiveness didn't happen over night. Tonight, he held her tighter than he'd ever done before. All her worries faded away.

She woke in the early hours, got out of bed and stood by the window. The moonlight was beautiful.

"What are you doing out of bed?" he asked, climbing out and walking over to her side.

"I couldn't sleep."

His hand swept over her shoulders and down her side.

"Max I'm sorry I fucked up... I hate myself for it all."

"Hey," he held her chin up. "You didn't fuck it up. You have given us a second chance – and that's all we need to make this work." He walked her back to the bed and made love to her one kiss at a time. They laid in the moonlight and Max's hand stroked up and down her belly.

"It used to bother me when you put your hand on my belly like that. It hurt deep inside, but now it feels like heaven. I'm so in love with you, Max – sometimes when I look at you, I forget how to breathe."

Max's hand faltered and she watched as a shadow flicked over his face.

"What is it?" she asked, not really wanting to hear the answer.

He shook his head. "Don't Susan, not now."

Susan sat up and pulled the covers around her defensively.

"Max, we need to talk. We're silently tearing each other apart."

Max didn't reply at first, and she saw how his eyes were filling with tears. The sight of it made her feel almost sick – what had she done to him?

"I'm sorry, Max – I wish I could travel back in time and make things right, but I can't."

"I know."

"Then I don't know what to do. I don't know how to make it better. Have you stopped loving me?" she asked.

Max shot her a look of hurt. "How can you ask that? It's because I love you that I'm here, by your side. I love you so much that I haven't given a thought to myself in months – that's what you do when you love someone as much as I love you," said Max.

"Susan took his hand in hers. "I really am sorry. I'm working on keeping things in the past, but I need you to look at me with that sparkle in your eye that you had on the beach the day I saw you … I need you to want me, not to look after me.

This is our future, Max. We both need to leave the past where it is."

He kissed her stomach and then her lips. "Then let's start making our future – right now. Susan, will you marry me?"

His question threw her for a moment. After what had just passed between them, it was the last thing she had expected. "I thought we were going to wait a little while?"

Max shifted himself up onto his elbow. "I don't want to wait; I want you, and this little one, to be mine..."

Smiling back at him she tilted he head. "Max you don't

need piece of paper to tell you that, we're already yours."

He noted the plural and smiled.

"Let's do it next month – while you can still fit into something slinky," he teased.

She giggled. "Okay, but let's go away for a couple of days first. I don't fancy our chances with Beth and Polly planning. Between all the baby shopping and wedding planning, I think we're going to need a little alone-time together first." She let out a quiet laugh snuggling herself into him.

He kissed her forehead, stroking her hair. "We have the rest of our life's together… Now let's get some sleep."

Chapter 12

(Three weeks later)

The weeks passed quickly. Susan stood in front of the long bedroom mirror looking down at her body. They'd been on a rollercoaster of emotions and come to the obvious conclusion that neither could survive without the other. What happened on this day would determine the future they both hoped for.

As she stood running her hand over her growing belly she could feel how much her bump had grown over the last month. Polly and Beth had been feeding her up and reading through the baby books like some crazed baby-police recruits.

Max had spent all his spare time by Susan's side, just like he promised.

"Max, come and look at this – do you think I'm starting to show?" she laughed, holding her t-shirt up.

He walked over to her, examining her. "Don't be daft, babe, you're only a few weeks.

"I'm like three months, now." As soon as she said it, she winced. Three months ago had been dark times.

"Anyway, we'd better be going if we want to make this scan appointment," he said, ignoring the statement. "Have you got your water!" he said, grabbing his keys.

Susan took the water and drank a large mouthful from the bottle.

When they arrived at the hospital the nurse took her

notes and told them to take a seat. Max took her hand and held it tight when the nurse called her name, instructing her to follow them. She instructed Susan to climb onto the bed and lift her top up. The nurse smiled at Max as she asked him if it was their first baby. He nodded and squeezed Susan's hand.

"Now this is going to feel a little cold," the nurse said, before squirting the jelly over Susan's belly. "Ah, not camera shy are we little one? There you go, mummy!" she said, tilting the screen Susan's way.

Susan saw the tiny fingers waving around and a tear slipped down her cheek. She turned Max and laughed when she saw he also had tears in his eyes.

"I can't believe it, baby," Max whispered in her ear.

The nurse paused the screen taking different measurements. "Now you're about eighteen weeks, do you want to know the sex?"

"Pardon? Did you say eighteen weeks? Susan asked.

"Well your measurements and baby development indicates your around eighteen weeks." Sensing the tension in the room, the nurse tentatively asked, "Is something wrong?" The nurse gave Max a worrying look.

Max and Susan gave each other a look as they both came to the same conclusion.

"We were in Paris!"

"Yes, baby, we were in Paris!" Max said grinning.

"Do you want to know the sex of the baby?" the nurse asked visibly relieved.

"No!" Susan snapped. "We wouldn't like to know the sex."

“That’s fine a lot of people like to keep it a surprise. Would you like a picture printing?”

Max took hold of Susan’s hand once more, clutching it tightly. “Yes, if that’s okay?”

The nurse cleaned Susan’s belly, covering her up in the process. “Yes, that’s fine. Just head to the nurse on the desk she will sort it out for you. You also need to book your next scan.”

Max helped her down and wrapped his arms around her waist. “Eighteen weeks, baby! I can’t believe it. I love you so much!”

All this time, all the fear about Max and children and she was already pregnant! How could she not have known? How did she miss the signs? Everything that she had put her baby through; the stress, the drink.

She clasped Max hand on the way to the car. “Max, I don't deserve any of this.”

“This is a new start,” she said, smiling.

When they arrived home, Max headed into the kitchen and put the kettle on. “Do you mind if I go for a walk?” she asked.

He looked at her quizzically, “Sure, that’s fine, I’ll come with you.”

“No,” she held her hand up to stop him “I just need to be alone for a few minutes. I won’t be long, I promise.” With that she headed out of the door. He called after her, “Are you okay, baby?” but she didn’t hear.

She contemplated walking to the beach, but instead she headed up the hill to the woods at the top. The cold wind cooled her thoughts. When she arrived at the woods it was even colder than she’d expected. The leaves crumbled beneath her feet. Autumn was knocking on the door. She took a seat on one of the picnic benches and looked out across to the sea in the distance. This place was home. The home where she would raise her own family with Max by her side.

Her phone buzzed in her pocket with a message from Polly. It was asking where she was. Apparently she was round at her house and was worried. She quickly texted her back, telling her she'd be back in a few minutes.

"Where have you been? What have you been doing?" Polly demanded.

"Whoa there, Poll, I just needed a little fresh air," Susan said, hanging her coat up. "You don't need to worry, I'm fine – I'm more than fine."

Max walked over to her and wrapped his arms around her. "Are you sure?

She smiled "Who wants a brew?"

Beth walked over and sat down at the table. "I'll have one, please." She winked at Susan conspiratorially. "I was thinking that as you're further along than what we thought, we should maybe go and do some baby shopping. What do you think?"

"That would be lovely, Beth, thank you." She kissed her on the cheek and whispered in her ear.

Beth gave her a smile. "You're welcome."

"Leave the coffee for me, I've got to go. I have a date!"

"What do you mean, a date? With who? Where are you going? And, why wasn't I told?" Susan couldn't get her questions out quick enough.

"Well you know Dillon at the garage?" Polly blushed.

Susan nodded curiously. "I dropped my car off at the garage the other day and he quizzed Max for my number. He rang me this morning."

Susan giggled. "Polly, he is like thirteen!"

"Twenty-four actually, and age is just a number." Polly tried to be serious but her smile gave it away.

"Okay, okay you're right! Just be safe and text me later with the details," Susan ordered, sipping her coffee.

"Well don't pass those details onto me, will you." Max said laughing. "I still have to work with him – and she better not eat him alive, good mechanics are hard to find."

Beth put her cup in the sink and walked over to Max hugging him tight. "I'm going to head back with Polly, I'm so pleased for you, son."

She looked at Susan with a tearful smile on her face. "Your mum would have been so proud of you; through all the dark and dismal times, you still managed to shine through. I just know the future is going to be blessed. "

Beth kissed her on the cheek before following Polly out of the door. "I'll see you tomorrow."

"Well, an evening alone, what do you want to do?"

"I'm going to run a bath. Pick a film for when I get back."

On the way to the bathroom, she couldn't resist taking a peep at the spare room that would soon become the nursery. She pictured where everything would go; the crib and the changing table, the rocking chair, she could even see the lemon colour of the walls. Something still tugged at her fears, deep inside, but she had to push them aside, they couldn't rule her anymore.

"Hey, are you asleep in there?" she had fallen so far into her thoughts she didn't initially hear Max knocking on the door.

Lifting herself out of the bath, she called out to him. "I'll be down in a minute."

Max was sat on the sofa with the laptop on his knee.

"Hey, what you looking at?" she tucked her self up next to him.

Max shut the screen and pushed the computer under the table. "Nothing really, just browsing. I made you tea."

Susan lifted her head up to look at him. "Max?"

"What, baby?" he stared at her waiting for her response.

Susan fidgeted with the hem of her satin nightdress. There was so much she wanted to tell him, so much to say, "It's nothing. I love you."

Max lent in a kissed her. "I love you too, baby, and I was thinking, why don't we get away for a couple of days, wherever you want to go?"

Smiling up at him her replied. "Are you sure?"

"Of course I'm sure, I think we deserve a break from everything; let's just get away and be us for a few days. No worries or problems, just us." He hugged her "Let's scrap the film and go to bed – what do you say?"

"Mmm, sounds good to me." Susan stood up holding her hand out for his. Max followed her lead, switching the lights off on his way out the room.

Susan woke early next morning. Creeping downstairs, she fired up the computer and went into the kitchen to prepare breakfast. After ten minutes of searching on the Internet she found the perfect weekend away for them. It was a quiet cabin for rent deep in the woods, by a lake. Pulling out her credit card, she booked the cabin and printed of the booking details off before heading upstairs to wake Max.

"Hey, sleepy, I brought you some breakfast," she whispered into his ear.

Max opened his eyes and sat up. "You didn't need to do this."

Susan smiled at him. "Yes I did." She waved a piece of paper in front of him. "I have a surprise for you."

"What's this?" Max asked, taking the piece of paper from her.

"It's a weekend away – this weekend; just you, me, bump and a cabin in the middle of nowhere."

Max examined the paper. "That sounds perfect!"

"I have another surprise." Susan couldn't contain her excitement. "I have been doing some digging this morning and found out that we can get married at the beach at the pagoda!"

"What? That's brilliant."

Giggling, Susan continued, "We just need a registrar to come and perform the service and I was thinking maybe we'd keep it small, just your mum, Polly and maybe a few other people you'd like.

"How long have you been up this morning" Max laughed pulling her under the cover with him.

"Only about an hour, Anyway, I'm thinking we need to book for next month or around that time, before the weather starts turning?"

"You're joking right? Next month? My mum and Polly are going to have a fit. This doesn't give them time to plan!" Max took hold of her hands. "Is this what you want?"

"Is this what you want, Max?" she longed to give him everything he deserved.

He flung his arms around her and pulled her into him. "Of course this is what I want!"

She tried to wriggle out of his grip but Max held on tight. "Max don't you think we should go and make some phone calls?"

Max pulled the cover back over their heads. "Nope, I think we should spend the day in bed." His finger traced her lips and down her neck onto her swelling breasts – she was helpless at his touch.

Trying to resist him she flung the covers back off them, giggling. "We can spend the whole weekend in bed, after we have made some calls – and after I have been baby shopping with Beth. I promised her."

Max sat up with a childlike expression of disappointment on his face. "Spoil sport! Will Polly be going too?"

"Nope," Susan shook her head. "I think young Dillon has stolen her heart – or something like that. I spoke to her this morning and she's spending the day with him. Your mum said she didn't't come home last night."

Max covered his ears. "Whoa there, too much information!"

From the shower, Susan heard the phone ring. When she came into the bedroom, Max hung up.

"Who was that on the phone?" she asked, rubbing her hair with the towel.

He kissed her on the check. "Work. I need to go in. There's a mix up with the suppliers. Sorry, baby but I've got to go and sort it out."

"Its okay, I'll be out with your mum; you can meet up with us when you're done." Susan began to walk down stairs when he grabbed her hand, pulling her back to him.

His hands wrapped around her cheeks. "Are we okay now, baby?"

"Hey, we're more than okay!"

Max gave her another kiss and skipped down the stairs. The doorbell rang and he opened it to see Beth, carrying a pile of letters.

"Hi, bye, gotta dash," he said, dashing past her.

"Love you too, son," she muttered.

"Go on in. Susan's dressing but she'll be down in a minute." He ran back and kissed Beth on the cheek before heading to the car.

Susan came down with her hair still damp. "Is everything okay, love?" Beth asked sweetly.

"Yeah, I think it is, Beth. I think they are more than okay." Susan took the cup Beth offered.

Susan looked at her and she was smiling.

"Drink up – we've got a lot of shopping to do!" Beth said.

Susan drank down, picked up her phone up and headed for the door.

Beth drove out to the next town, which had a large toy and baby shop. When the car pulled into the parking space, Susan realised Beth hadn't been joking when she had said the place was huge. Beth beamed with excitement as she grabbed one of the big trolleys and went inside. Susan laughed and followed.

Beth wasted no time, heading straight for the baby clothes and picking up several packs of vests and baby grows all in cream and yellow colours,

"You need to be practical. You'll be amazed how many you'll get through."

Then she led Susan to the bottles. "Have you given any thought to feeding? Are you breastfeeding? I mean it's entirely up to you but you'll need some equipment whichever you choose."

Susan's face reddened a little as she shrugged her shoulders

"Well they say 'breast is best', but in all honestly it's all down to baby and mummy, so we can get some bottles and formula closer to the time when we've seen how it's gone. " Beth took hold of the trolley, smiling. Susan had no idea about any of the things she needed.

Beth had almost filled the trolley with all the 'essentials' needed; there were blankets, towels, creams, nappies and clothes, along with a changing table and feeding chair and some cute decorating border with little teddy bears on for the nursery. Beth got a store helper to help transfer from the store to the car.

Susan's phone went off in her handbag. It was Max. She smiled and answered it. After a brief chat, she relayed the situation to Beth, "Unfortunately Max can't make it; he says he'll meet us at home instead."

"Its okay, sweetie we'll call it a day. You look tired and I think we've both had enough for today.

Chapter 13

Susan sat quietly on the way home; she had wanted Max to be there when they had picked the baby things, and she felt a little sad that he'd had to work. When they got back, his car was parked in the drive. Beth gave a little toot of the horn and Max came out waving. He was still in his overalls from the garage, his hair was scuffed up and grease marks were streaked across his forehead.

"Sorry I couldn't make it, baby. I ended up having to sort a job out." He fluttered his eyelashes and pouted his lips before pinching her bottom.

"Put her down," Beth jested, passing him the bags. "She doesn't want your greasy hands all over her."

Little did Beth know that's exactly were Susan wanted his hands – all over her body. Despite being a little bit mad that he'd not been there, she still couldn't resist. She shook the thought out of her mind and headed inside the house to put the kettle on while Beth and Max continued carrying the many boxes and bags in from the car. Susan checked through the post. The bottom letter had been sent to Beth's by mistake and she'd brought it with her, dumping it on the pile of post. Instinctively, Susan had a strange feeling about the letter. The envelope had a pastel blue tinge to it and the return address was to a woman called Isabelle Blake. It looked personal.

"Anything interesting?" Max's arms wrapped around her waist.

Susan paused for a moment then held the letter out to

him. “Just this one.” She tried to resist asking but couldn’t. “Who is Isabelle?” She tried to mask her curiosity by laughing a little but Beth’s reaction only made her feel worse. The moment Susan had said the name, Beth’s face looked as though she had seen a ghost. “Max is there something you need to tell me?” she turned to him and stared at him seriously.

Quickly, he folded the letter and pushed it in to his back pocket. “It’s nothing, baby.” He shook his head but there was an uncomfortable look in his eye. “She’s just someone who used to live near us, that’s all.” He glanced at his mum.

Beth gave Susan a kiss on the cheek. “I’m going to get home. Thanks for today. I had a lovely time, sweetheart.”

Max followed Beth out to the car and Susan watched them from the window. Something felt wrong. Max and Beth appeared to be arguing. All at once, Beth threw her arm in the direction of the house and Susan.

‘Surely Beth must have recognised the name on the letter? Why did she bring it over? What was she trying to do?’ Susan pondered.

Max crossed his arms and headed back to the house looking subdued.

Susan could seem him pulling the letter out of his pocket; he ripped it open and looked at it for a second before throwing it into the bin. He looked back at the house and gave Susan a smile. But when he opened the door Susan stormed off into the kitchen, slamming the cups around.

“What’s going on, Max, I know you’re hiding something?”

Max sat at the table twiddling his fingers then took a breath. “Okay sit down before you break something and I’ll tell you.”

Susan didn’t speak, she just sat at the opposite end of the table and glowered at him, waiting for his explanation.

“Okay – Isabelle is an ex-girlfriend who I dated when we finished school. We broke up and she moved away. I haven’t heard from her since she left.” Max brushed his fingers through his hair.

“Bull shit!” Susan shot up from her seat. “You’re not telling me everything. I saw the way Beth reacted, and the way you and her were outside. There is more to this than you’re telling me, Max so don’t fucking patronise me… tell me the truth now!”

“Susan, please just sit down. I haven’t heard from her since she left – not until now.” He held on to Susan’s hands across the table. “Listen, it’s complicated; we went out for over two years and we got engaged but then I found out she had been sleeping with someone else behind my back; next thing I called the whole thing off and the two of them left town together “

“That’s all?” Susan’s foot tapped against the table leg impatiently.

His head dropped a little. “No, about a year after she left, she got in touch saying she’d had a little boy and that I could be the father. My mum insisted we did a DNA test before I had any further communication with her. It was a good job too because it wasn’t mine. After that I didn’t hear anything from her, and I don’t want to.”

“This is a big thing, Max; how could you keep it from me after everything we went through? After everything we have said about honesty. Does that mean nothing to you? And what the hell does she want?" Susan stood up and walked over to the sink.

Max`s hands stroked down her arms. "Just let it go, baby, I don't want to fight with you over this... I don't want you upsetting yourself over *this*."

Susan walked away from his touch. "No, Max I'm sorry but I need answers. Why did you hide this from me? You can't really expect me to let this go?"

"The reason I didn't tell you is because I didn't think it mattered. Do you want to know about all my ex-girlfriends? We went out. She cheated and left, what more is there to know?"

Susan slammed her cup onto the table. "Fuck you, Max! It's more than that; you were fucking engaged to her. Why would you keep that from me? More to the point, what are you hiding now? What the fuck does the letter say?" What was he hiding from her; she thought she knew everything about him but she didn't like this side to him at all.

She stormed out of the door to the bin, pulled the letter out and stormed back inside, slamming it onto the table. Tears streamed down her face. She read the letter and she got angry. "Why the hell would she want to meet up with you?"

"Susan, please, just calm down. You're not doing yourself any favours getting worked up over nothing. Please, I threw it away because I don't want anything to do with her!"

"Really!"

Max slammed his hand onto the table with frustration. You know what, fuck it… if you can't understand that...

then I'm out of here. It's never enough. I'm not enough." He slammed the door behind him.

Susan stood at the window watching the rain. When she was sure that he was out of sight, she headed across the yard to the bin and pulled out the torn envelope, reading the number under the address. Before she knew what she was doing, she punched the number into her phone and waited for the voice to answer. She needed to hear what this woman sounded like. The phone was answered with a weary "hello!" Susan hadn't thought any of it through and was left gaping like a fish on the end. Eventually she croaked, "hello" and introduced herself as Max's fiancée. The other person abruptly hung up. She curled up on the sofa and waited. It wasn't long before she heard a tap at the door. It was Max and he was soaked through.

"Can I come in, please?"

Wiping the tears from her eyes she nodded.

"Listen, baby, I really don't want to fight. The reason I didn't tell you is because I was hurt by her and I didn't want you to feel sorry for me – I wanted you to have confidence in me; to think that I was strong. And I threw the letter away because I don't want to know what she has to say. Please, can we just forget about it?" he asked trying to get her to make eye contact with him.

"Max, you shouldn't have kept it from me."

"I'm sorry. Can't we just forget this who mess, baby?"

Susan sat for a moment lost in her hurt and thoughts.

Mistaking her silence, he started to walk out of the room. "Wait!" She jumped up "I'm sorry. I understand."

He nodded. "Don't be. I really wouldn't hurt you." Max kissed her forehead. "Now let's get this stuff upstairs."

Max picked up the box and carried it upstairs.

As Max lugged the boxes up into the loft, she set about making a cup of tea. A text message pinged on her phone; the number read unknown. The text read, "Can we talk?" Her heart quickened. She knew exactly who it was. She snuck outside into the garden and dialed the number.

"Hello?" the women's voice answered.

Susan, not wanting to exchange pleasantries, darted straight to the point. "Why do you want to see Max?"

The line was silent for a moment before the women responded, "Why I want to see Max has nothing to do with you!"

Susan felt her anger rising. "Now you listen to me! I'm his fiancée and I'm carrying his baby, so it has everything to do with me."

The women cackled, "Oh, Sweetie, you silly girl, all I need to do is click my fingers and he'd come running back. He can't resist me! He never could. I know just how to make him tick."

Susan paced to the bottom of the garden. "Who the hell do you think you are? Max has told me about you. I know all about your so-called charms; you're nothing but a slapper that tried to ruin his life. Well guess what? He wants nothing to do with you."

The phone went dead, leaving Susan unnerved. *'He couldn't resist her he never could.'* Had Max been telling her the whole truth? She felt there was more to the story: more he was hiding.

"Hey, who are you talking to out here?" Max asked from the doorway.

Susan jumped and stuffed the phone back into her

pocket. “No one, I was just trying to get hold of Polly.”

Max crossed his arms over his chest and pulled his shoulders back. “She’s inside! Said she tried calling you but couldn’t get through.”

“I bet we both tried ringing at the same time,” Susan lied, walking past him into the kitchen to a chirpy Polly making coffee.

“Hey Poll.”

“Hi, yourself. How’s bump?”

Susan gave a weak smile and stroked her tummy. “Good.”

“Excellent news. Feeling alright? You look a bit peaky?”

“Sickness is a mare. Actually, I could really do with some fresh air – fancy a walk?” Susan asked, raising her eyebrows in secret communication.

Polly put her spoon down, “Yeah, sure! We’ll have a cuppa when we get back then.”

They left Max looking slightly bemused. Susan hadn’t mentioned anything about feeling sick all morning. He liked Polly a lot, he’d always respect her for looking after Susan during the dark times, but it didn’t stop the sense of jealousy he felt about their closeness; he knew that they’d be talking about the letter.

As soon as they were out of the sight of the house, Polly stopped Susan in her tracks. “Okay, what is up? You’re acting really weird”

Susan took a deep breath. “Oh, Polly, why is my life always so complicated?”

Polly laughed, “Because you mostly make it complicated, honey. What’s happened now?”

"Max got a letter from an ex earlier. When I asked him about it, we ended up in an argument and he walked out. I couldn't help myself, I called her."

"Oh, Susan!" Polly groaned. "Why?"

"Yeah, I know – possibly not the smartest move, but I couldn't help it!" She sat down on a bench, her legs aching from the walk up the hill. "When I rang her and told her to leave him alone she laughed at me. She told me I was stupid to think she couldn't get him back. She said he could never resist her. I think he's hiding more from me."

Polly put her arm around her. "Are you sure she isn't just a jealous ex that's pissed off? Because that's what it sounds like to me."

"I don't know Poll, she sounded so sure of her self; like all she needed to do was click her fingers and he would go running."

"Susan, I'm sure it's nothing. He only has eyes for you and this little one." Her hand stretched over Susan's tummy.

Susan looked down taking the moment in. Polly would always be here to put things right to lead her in the right direction. "Yeah you're right I'm just over reacting, what would I do without you?"

Polly let out a laugh. "You'd be alright."

"Hmm, I'm not so sure."

"Anyway," Polly said, changing direction, "I came to talk to you about Dillon."

"Oh, I'm so sorry Poll, I'm such a crappy friend - I haven't even asked you about your date or anything. How did it go?"

"Well, I think I'm a little more experienced than him, if

you know what I mean! It's all a little Mrs. Robinson."

"Hot!" Susan interrupted.

Polly nudged her playfully on the arm, "But I really like him and we have a great time together. Just then, the sky opened and large raindrops fell. "Come on, I'll tell you more when we get back to your house. It's going to pour it down."

The two of them walked arm in arm. Susan was comforted by Polly's thoughts on the matter. She was right about Isabelle; she was just a jealous ex looking for a reaction. Susan had given her just what she was looking for.

In two days Max and her would be alone together – no one else to interrupt them. They would be alone to be a proper couple with no stress and no complications. Susan had big plans for the weekend. Plans that involved reconnecting both mentally and physically. News of the baby, and all the complications around it had really got between them, and not just emotionally.

When they arrived back at the house, Max was sat in the office. "Hey, Max, do you want a cuppa?" Susan asked.

"Can you come here a minute, baby?" Max replied. Susan gave Polly a quick smile and left her to making the coffee.

"What's up Max?" she asked, stretching her arm over his shoulder and giving him a quick kiss on the cheek.

Max spun around in his office chair and faced her, crossing his arms over his chest and giving her a serious stare. "Are you sure everything is good between us?"

"Sure," she nodded, "Why wouldn't it be?"

"I thought you might still be mad with me, what with

you going for a walk with Polly."

Susan gave a sigh of relief. "Yeah, Max we're fine! We won't be if you keep asking though." He looked at her and sighed. "Okay," he said raising his hand.

"Anyway what are you up to?" she asked deflecting.

Max turned the computer screen in her direction to show her a beautiful hotel on the screen.

"I've seen that place before," she said. "It's just out of town. Why are you showing me this?"

"Well," he pulled Susan onto his lap, wrapping his arms around her. "This is where we are going to spend our wedding night. We'll have our wedding on the beach and then head over to this place for a meal, and then we'll spend the night there – just the three of us."

Susan's mouth fell open into a big smile. "Max, I don't know what to say."

He pulled her mouth down to his and kissed her. She could feel the passion in it and wished that they were in the house alone. Her body ached for him. He pulled away from her. "I have another surprise."

Her hand stroked his thigh and she felt him stiffen under her touch. "Yes, you have!" she purred.

He giggled into her neck. "Easy tiger!"

"I can't help it – it's the hormones!" she pouted.

"Anyway, that's not the surprise I'm on about – I spoke with the registrar and she can fit us in in six weeks on the twelfth."

"Oh, my God, Max!" she squealed. "That's amazing. The twelfth – that's going to be our wedding day!"

Hearing all the commotion, Polly poked her head around the door.

"Hey, what's all the excitement?"

Susan turned to her. "Max has set the date with the registrar – the twelfth of next month!"

Max tipped her off her knee and spun his chair around. "Off you go – go and talk flowers or something, I've got work to do," he said, laughing.

They headed back into the kitchen, Susan dancing in a cloud of giddiness.

"Whoa, the twelfth of next month – that's soon. How are you going to organise a wedding in that time?"

Susan's smile dropped into a pout. "Well I was hoping you would be helping me out on the planning, being chief bridesmaid and all that."

Polly had a tear in her eye. "Oh, my little sister all grown up!"

Susan noted the term little sister and smiled. Yes, that's exactly what Polly was, she was the sister she never had. It felt wonderful that she had defined it at last.

"Polly," she held her hand to her chest. "You *are* my sister and I love you."

"I love you to. And Max – I know I've had some doubts, but never about him, Susan; Max and you are perfect together."

Max walked in beaming with joy. His eyes sparkled when they met Susan's.

Polly, suddenly feeling a bit of gooseberry, smiled and headed towards the door,

"Anyway, honey, I'm going to go. I'm meeting up with Dillon for… for drinks." She winked and Susan laughed. "You two have fun celebrating. I'll talk to Beth later about organizing your hen night."

Susan grabbed hold of her arm. “Please, no fuss; I have everything I need right here.” Her eyes darted around the room from Polly to Max and back to Polly.

Polly gave a little nod. “Okay then, see ya later!”

Chapter 14

The cold weather had crept in. Susan wrapped herself up on the couch. Max had left for work early that morning and Susan had the whole day to herself with nothing to do. Polly and Beth had taken control of the wedding arrangements, for which she was very grateful, and she was looking forward to a day resting – getting herself ready for their weekend away starting tomorrow. She was so looking forward to it.

The whole Isabelle letter had really shaken things up between them; it had been so out of the blue and unexpected. Neither had spoken about it since yesterday afternoon and she was happy to put it behind her. She hadn't told Max that she'd phoned Isabelle. She knew that would not go down well. Hungry, she threw the cover off and headed to the kitchen to make lunch. When she opened the fridge, she saw Max's packed lunch box still on the shelf. It would make a good excuse to make a visit, she thought.

She put her coat on and headed out the door with the intention of gatecrashing his lunchtime. The walk to the garage felt further than usual but then again she was more pregnant than the last time she made the walk.

She walked in and saw Dillon glance at her nervously. He was in the garage alone. There was no sign of Max anywhere.

"Where is Max?"

At first he tried to shrug as if he didn't know but Susan put her hand on her hip and gave him the death stare.

Dillon pointed to the cafe across the street.

"He went out for lunch, some chick wanted him to show her where to get a cuppa from."

Susan walked into the office and placed the lunch-box on the desk. "Oh some chick did! Did she? And what did this chick look like, Dillon?"

"I didn't really take any notice," he lied. "Blonde I think, and tall." Dillon fidgeted with the wrench he was holding. "Look, Max is a good man, maybe you shouldn't be busting his balls so much." Dillon said, looking awkward.

Susan glared at him but didn't answer. She left, feeling the rage building up inside her. She thought about storming into the cafe and demanding to know what was going on. It was obvious it was Isabelle. Instead, she hovered outside the cafe window looking for him. He was smiling, almost laughing. She couldn't see the woman's face but she could see her long blonde hair. She watched as Max took a sip of his coffee, his eyes fixed on the women. Her heart sank when he leant forward and kissed her on the cheek, but the women turned her head and their lips locked together. She walked away empty and hurt.

As she reached the top of the hill, the pain was too much for her to bear. Her head felt lighter and the air around her vanished until there was none left. Reaching for the nearest bench, she pulled out her phone and dialed his number. "No!" she murmured, slamming the phone next to her. The pain in her chest worsened; her eyes shut then opened again to a stranger leaning over her. She pulled her eyes tight shut again, but this time they wouldn't open again.

Max rushed to the hospital as quickly as he could. Polly and Beth were following behind him but when he reached the desk they wouldn't let him to see her.

"Why the fuck won't you tell me what is going on? I want to see her now!" His fists slammed down on the counter.

The petite dark haired nurse stood up from her chair and stared hard at him, "Sir, if you don't calm down, I will have to call security."

Beth grabbed hold if his arm pulling him to the waiting area and said in a low voice, "Come on, Son."

"Why won't they let me see her, Mum? No one is telling me anything." His put his head in his hands.

A doctor walked over with a clipboard in his hand. "Is one of you Polly?" The young man looked at each of them.

Polly quickly stood up, "I am!"

"Would you like to follow me, please?" He was already walking down the corridor.

Max and Beth stood up and followed behind but when they reached the door, the doctor held out his hand. "I'm sorry, she only wants to see Polly."

"What the hell do you mean? I want to know what is going on!"

Polly's hand rested on his shoulder and he shook it off. "Max, calm down, I'll find out what's going on. You get a coffee and I'll sort it."

Max didn't't respond. He glared at Polly. *'Always fucking Polly!'* he thought. He dropped his head down and walked off down the corridor. Polly took a deep breath and opened the door. Susan lay in the bed. On seeing her, a small smile appeared.

"She needs to stay in over night, but she will be fine. She just needs to rest from now on. She shouldn't be getting agitated up like she did." The doctor nodded his head and left the room.

Polly took a seat next to the bed and gripped Susan's hand tightly. "What have you been getting yourself into now?"

Susan forced a smile but a tear trickled down her cheek. "I caught them, Poll. I saw them together!"

"What do you mean you *caught them together*?"

"I went to take Max some lunch, but he was at the cafe holding HER hand, he kissed her! He was laughing and smiling!" Susan couldn't control her anger.

Polly's face went white. "No! He wouldn't do that. Maybe you got it wrong?"

"I'm not wrong Poll, it was her! Isabelle. Who else would he be kissing in the cafe?"

Polly wrapped her arms around Susan's neck and hugged her. "It's okay, baby girl, sshh," she soothed, stroking Susan's hair.

"I don't want to see him. I just want him gone and out of my life for good. This whole thing has been a mess since it started. He isn't the man I thought he was, and never will be!" Susan snuggled her head down into the fluffy pillow.

"You get some sleep, I'll go back to yours and pick up some stuff." Polly stood. "You just rest and I'll be back soon."

Susan nodded off, drifting off into a deep sleep. Polly watched for moment. She was angry – more than she'd ever been. She set of to find Max to get some answers.

She approached Max, charging up to him like an angry bull, "YOU! I want a word with you, NOW!" Polly stood firm, her finger pointed in Max`s direction.

Max stood up from the table and his face whitened. "What is it? What's going on? How is she?" His nerves twitched.

"She is fine, she just needs rest and no stress. She doesn't want to see you anymore, Max. You two are over!" Polly's said firmly. She turned her back in him and walked out the main entrance.

"What do you mean we are over? What the fuck is going on?"

"She saw you, Max, with her, Isabelle, yeah! She saw you in the cafe... Kissing her. You've broken her heart, Max. I guessed you always would." Polly tilted her head to the side, waiting for his response.

Disbelief washed over his face, his eyes fell dark. "Let me explain, please!"

"She doesn't want to know, Max. You lied and you blew it. I really hoped you were different, but deep down you let her down just like everyone else. I trusted you to be there for her, to protect her and love her. You did nothing but give her false hope." Polly shrugged of his touch and walked away.

"Wait, wait, please!" Max begged, chasing her across to the car.

Beth ran after him, grabbing him by the arm and spinning him around. "Tell me it's not true, Max – you've got a baby on the way! You're going to be a father."

Max turned to her with tears in his eyes, "It's not true,

Mum, honestly, it's not, please believe me."

In the hospital bed, Susan stared out of the window and contemplated what the future held for her. She placed her hand softly around her tummy. She knew what she had to do, she had to be strong and stand alone. For the sake of the tiny treasure growing inside her, she had to carry on. Everything they had planned together was washed away in the image of him holding that woman's hand, of Max's lips on those of another woman.

A nurse came in the room and left a tray of food on the table, instructing her to eat something. Pushing the tray away, she sunk back into the pillow. She shed no tears for her broken relationship; the heartache didn't hurt, all that was left was emptiness, a deep, dark emptiness never to be filled again. He had taken her broken life and rebuilt it only to shatter every piece.

A small tap at the door snapped her from her thoughts. Beth's head peered around the doorway. "I didn't know if you would speak to me or not?"

Susan pulled herself up in the bed. "Of course I want to speak to you. Come in. It's Max I don't want to see at the minute. I can't face him."

"I understand that this has something to do with Max and Isabelle."

Susan flinched. Hearing their names together made them sound like a couple; as if Beth saw them that way too – maybe she still did.

"You have got understand that he would never jeopardize his relationship with you. Not now, not with the baby on the way." Beth struggled to hold back the tears.

"But he did, Beth; he held her hand in the café and he

was laughing. His eyes were all sparkly – I know the way he was looking at her, it was the way he used to look at me. I spoke to her on the phone and she told me she could have him whenever she wanted. That's just what she did. She came by and clicked her fingers and Max caved in like a little boy."

"She's playing tricks with you both and you have given her what she wanted." Beth said taking Susan's hand. "My son loves you with every inch of his heart and soul. He would never do anything to hurt you."

Susan rolled her eyes.

"I know what Isabelle is like; I've seen the hold she possessed over him – believe me, he feels nothing for her now. She broke his heart."

"She still has that hold over him, Beth."

"Susan, please - everything you two have been through; all you have gained and you're willing to throw it all away?"

Susan shook her head. "It's over, Beth. I'm sorry but he betrayed me."

Beth stood up and walked to the door. "Just promise me that you will think things over. I'll keep Max out your way for a few days to give you some space and time to think things over."

Susan was left alone with her thoughts. She couldn't make sense of anything. Climbing out of bed, she hunted around her handbag and dug her phone out. She asked Polly to pack up his things and take them to Beth's; she couldn't go back with memories of him everywhere. After the call ended, she pulled the cover over her head and drifted off to a dreamless sleep.

Max sat at his desk in the garage with his head in his hands. The realization of what had happened at the hospital still hadn't sunk in. He had sent her countless text messages and tried calling but it kept going straight to voice mail. He decides that he would go and see her tomorrow. He was sure that when she saw him she would have to listen to him – listen to what really happened.

"Well look who's drinking alone! Fancy some company?" The sound of stiletto heels on concrete sent shivers down his neck.

"What the fuck do you want? His voice was hollow and groggy. Max was not in the mood for any of Isabelle's games. "Just get out, Izzy!"

"Oh, Max, you know I can't do that." Her voice sounded almost vindictive. "I need you just as much as you need me."

Max looked at her – the picture-perfect women he had stupidly fell in love with. "You mean nothing to me now, Isabelle? You're not wanted around here. Don't you remember why you left here in the first place?"

Isabelle's hands pressed firm on his shoulders as he stared into his empty whiskey glass.

"You know why I'm here, Max! I came to tell you that I made a mistake. I want the three of us to be a family. You, me and Isaac."

"Get your hands off me!" Max jumped out of his seat and brushed her hands off his shoulders. "You have no right coming here and trying to fuck things up for me. What happened Izzy? Which guy let you down this time? You think just because you screwed things up with your bloke that you can come here and destroy what I have."

He slammed his glass down onto the desk and threw more whiskey into the glass. "You mean nothing to me, Izzy. You shagged my best friend behind my back and then expected me to just open my arms and welcome you back! You really are a bitch aren't you?"

"Max, I see you still have that fire in your pit, let me put it out for you." She pressed her lips together and slowly walked towards him. "Does she know about the things we did? How good we were together! I bet it's all vanilla sex and roses now... I bet she can't fulfill your desires – does she know just how dark and kinky you are, Max? Have you shown her your toys yet? You always were better in bed when you were angry. So rough and dirty."

He slammed the glass down once more. "You made me that way; you were the one who fucked me up, Izzy. You made me think that love wasn't enough. Just go home to your son and leave me alone. If you hadn't sent that letter then none of this would have happened."

Isabelle stopped. "It wasn't the letter that brought me here, it was her phone call." The grin on her face grew bigger with spite. "You don't know about the phone call I had with your dear sweet Susan. She is so insecure. It really isn't attractive!"

"What phone call? What have you done?" Max gripped her by the arms almost shaking her. "What have you said to her?"

"Max let go, you're hurting me." Her arms throbbed were his grip tightened. "Max, let go."

He pulled her closer until they were nose to nose. "Leave now and don't come back! EVER!" He pushed her away and walked back to his desk. She came up behind him and her hand ran through his hair, pulling his head back.

"You know I like it when you take control, Max! But I like it more when I'm in charge..." Her fingers pulled at his hair tighter, sending shockwaves down to his stomach. Her fingers traced his jaw line. His body couldn't help but respond – he had been trained that way.

Max pushed her hands off his face. "You fucked up. That way won't work anymore... I'm not under your sick spell anymore." Once more he came nose to nose with her. "You don't own me anymore, Izzy and you never will."

"You remember how good it felt; the pleasure we felt together? We could have that again, Max. All you have to do is say the magic word... come on, you know you want to…" Her lips pressed onto his, but despite the raging heat burning in him, Max didn't respond. His arms came up and pushed her out of the way, sending her toppling into the chair behind her.

Wiping his lips with the back of his hand, his voice came out like thunder. "I will never say *that* word to you again. You are a monster. You've a screw lose; you wouldn't know love if it bit you on the ass. What's wrong, Izzy, hubby not liking you play dominatrix. Won't he kneel on all fours for you and worship you? You may have owned me once, Isabelle, but not anymore: you can't be loved..."

Her hands flew up over her ears. "SHUT UP! SHUT UP! You will beg for me to come back, Max! Mark my words, when you crave her fingers scraping down your back, or her teeth tightening on your chest, or the sound of a whip crack, you'll think of me – she won't do those thing to you, Max... but I will, and I'll be waiting for you!"

Max charged at her, grabbing hold of her chin hard. "You will never touch me again, bitch! I never want to see you again. You need to leave town, and if I have to tell you again you will find out just how much I really do despise you. Now get the fuck out my garage you sad pathetic freak!"

Isabelle stood breathing deep and hard. His eyes washed over her with disgust, not the obedience they once had. Susan had won...

"Fine, Max, I'll go, but you know she won't take you back – not now. Even if she did, she'll ruin you. Just remember, I gave you the chance of what you wanted and you turned it down."

The sound of her shoes scurrying away echoed through the garage. He tried Susan's phone once more but there was still no answer. With his whiskey glass empty and his heart in pieces, he left the garage and staggered to his mum's house. He let himself in with the spare key and headed to his old room. He slumped on the bed and cried.

He thought back to the time Isabelle was in his life, the destruction she had caused; she had changed him. Almost broken him...

The smell of her overpowering perfume still lingered on his clothes. How could so much change in one single day? He still had no idea what happened with Susan or if she was okay. Nothing made sense to him anymore. Isabelle had such a hold over him, it burnt his skin deep.

He got up and went into the bathroom – he wanted to wash every single bit of that vindictive bitch off his body. Earlier that day she'd swung by and managed to dig her claws in, suckering him into her sob story about her husband not loving her and son away being taken away from her. Max had felt sorry for her.

He stood in front of the mirror staring at his own sad reflection. He unbuttoned his shirt and turned the shower on to a blistering heat – he felt the need to purge his skin and his sin.

Thoughts rumbled like thunder through his head. His fists hit the shower wall so hard that he cracked the tiles under his fist. Tiny drops of blood fell to the floor where they mingled with the water and washed away. Max felt broken, beat and empty. Nothing would fill the hole until she lay next to him again.

Chapter 15

Days turned into weeks. Susan grew used to the feeling of not having Max around. She hadn't spoken to him since the day she finished everything. She still yearned for his touch but she couldn't give in. Polly had removed all his things and she had moved in with her to look after her and the baby. It had allowed Max to move back in with his mother. Now six months pregnant, Susan faced an unknown future but she was stronger now, strong enough to face it.

"Hey mummy," Polly snuck into the bedroom tiptoeing to the bed with a cup in hand. "I made you a chamomile tea..."

Susan pulled the covers off her head. "Poll you know I hate that stuff, it tastes like crap. What's wrong with a proper cup of tea once and a while?" Susan pulled her face sitting up.

"Up and at them, honey, let's get ready to go and see that not-so-little bump of yours. Beth is downstairs and she's getting impatient." Polly jumped up and down on the bed like it was Christmas morning.

"Okay, okay, just go wait downstairs while I grab a shower, I'll be down in a minute." Susan pulled herself out of the bed and dragged her feet to the bathroom. She'd changed a lot of things since Max, her hair was now short, in a bob, her nails neatly manicured, her maternal curves had softened and changed her body, and she felt beautiful for the first time in her life. She finished showering and searched for something suitable to wear. Today was her second scan and the doctors wanted to make sure everything was going well since her collapse. Her heart stopped when she rummaged through the top draw and her hand found a box. She picked it up and sat on the end of the bed pulling the lid up; inside was the necklace Max had given her. Sadness flooded over her.

Beth gave a small tap at the door and peered her head around the corner. "Sweetie? Are you almost ready to go?" She still felt unsure how she should be around Susan. After everything that had happened, she didn't know her place anymore. Susan had said from the start that nothing had changed between them, that bump would still need a grandma, but so much had changed. She'd spent the last few weeks, watching her son spiral out of control, taking his father's hard-built business with him. It broke her heart to see the two people she loved walk down different paths knowing they should be hand in hand together.

"Hey, Beth. Yeah, I'm ready. How are you?" Susan pushed the old memory back into its box and headed over to Beth to give her a hug. "I'm so glad you could make it, it means so much to me."

Beth hung onto the hug longer than was needed, but she needed to know that everything was okay. "I wouldn't miss it for the world. I get to see my grandchild for the first time! I couldn't sleep last night with excitement."

"Come on then, you two, let's get moving before we're late." Polly shouted from the bottom of the stairs.

Beth led the way down. Picking her coat up on the way, she climbed into the car with a sparkle in her eye for the first time in weeks.

Max reached the top of Susan's street just as the car turned the corner. He caught a glimpse of the women he loved smiling alongside his mother. He was too late, she had already moved on. She had changed her mobile and home phone number, ensuring that his midnight begging calls could no longer get through. As much as he felt sad, he felt angry. She had no right cutting him out of his baby's life; it was his baby too, not just hers. He'd nothing wrong and if she would only listen to him she would find out the truth about that day, but she wouldn't. Several times the wicked thought that Susan had used him crept across his mind. She'd only ever really wanted a baby, and Max was nothing more than a donor.

He sat down on her front step and held his head in his hands. He knew that that wasn't true. She had loved him. He was certain that she couldn't just forget that. He was losing everything. He'd sold his car in exchange for a bike, a Harley in fact. He hardly spent any time at home or the garage, but at a bar outside of town full of bikers. Here he could be away from judgment; his mother had always been good at that. He drank, he smoked and he tried to forget. He was an entirely different man to the man he was six weeks ago. He'd even paid a drink-influenced visit to the out of town tattooist and coming back with a full sleeve. The pain had been delicious and he hadn't been able to stop his thoughts playing with images of Isabelle.

He pulled the half-bottle of whiskey from his pocket.

"Okay, here we go. Baby is doing great! Does mummy want to know the sex?" the nurse asked, turning the screen for Susan to get a better view.

Susan looked at Beth and Polly. “Yes,” she nodded, “I think I’d like to know?” She’d thought about it all night and decided that now she was on her own she needed to get as much ready as possible.

“Well let’s have a look, there you go you see this here?” the nurse pointed to a small blur on the screen. “This is his… well… it’s a boy!”

“Oh, Susan, a boy!" Polly squeezed Susan’s hand. Beth had tears in her eyes as she looked at the screen.

The nurse continued with the scan moving round Susan’s belly. She hesitated and looked confused. She returned to the previous spot and paused the screen. “I won’t be a moment, I just need to speak to the doctor.

Susan started to panic. What’s wrong? Why do you need the doctor? You just said everything was fine… what’s going on?” The nurse had already left the room. “Beth what’s happening?”

“I have no idea, sweetie, let’s just calm down and wait to see what she says.” Beth held Susan’s hand tightly. There was a sharp tap at the door and a short stocky women in a white coat entered the room, rubbing her hands together.

“Okay, mummy, let’s just have a look at this.”

“What’s going on? The nurse wouldn’t tell me what is happening. Is my baby okay?” Susan had tears in her eyes. *Twenty-four weeks – that’s when it happened the last time. What if I’m losing the baby?*

“Everything is fine with your baby, Susan – you have nothing to worry about. The nurse just wanted to check something with me – standard procedure.

"What?"

The Doctor pointed to a blur in the background. "This little one has been hiding behind her brother. That's why she didn't show up on the previous scan. She's been ducking out of our way."

"WHAT? You mean..." Susan didn't know what to say.

"Yes," the doctor smiled at Susan. "it's twins. Now the little girl in the background is slightly smaller than we would like, and she is very camera shy so we would like to see you again in about five weeks for another scan, and then you will have to make frequent visits to the anti-natal clinic for checkups, but everything's looking good at the moment. Do you have any questions?"

She had a million questions but she couldn't speak. Beth cleared her throat,

"What will happen when she is due? Will she have a normal delivery?"

"Well, at the moment with the second baby being on the small side it's something we will have to monitor and speak about when we are closer to the time. I'm going to be your doctor from now on and if you have any worries you can come and speak to me about anything."

Shaking Susan's hand, she left the room, leaving the nurse cleaning Susan up from the cold jelly. "Best of both worlds, aren't you lucky?"

"Susan are you okay, honey?"

"I'm not sure, Polly, I don't know what to think." Susan hung onto Polly's hand and pulled herself off the bed.

Beth wrapped her coat around Susan's shoulders. "Let's just get you home. You need time for all of this to sink in – everything is going to be wonderful you'll see." Beth was bursting with excitement at the thought of two grandchildren to spoil.

The three of them walked silently to the car. Polly sat in the back with Susan. Beth drove them home and no one said a word.

The car pulled up onto the drive. Max was still sat on the front door step, swaying from the alcohol. Beth flashed Polly a look in the rear view mirror and, said, “Stay here, I’ll deal with it.”

She slammed the door hard behind her.

“Max? What are you doing here? You really need to go! This is really not a good idea.”

His slowly lifted up his head. His eyes were red like fire from where he had been crying. “Mum, I don’t want to go anywhere. I want to see her…” The words slurred out of his mouth.

“BETH! What’s going on? What is it?” Susan shouted, climbing out of the car.

Beth pulled Max to his feet. “Son, you really need to go – this is not a good time.”

“Why? Is something wrong?”

Max loosened from her grip. Stumbling to find his feet. “I just want to see her, mum and you can’t stop me…” He pushed past here and Beth flashed Susan an apologetic look.

“No, but I can!” Susan said sternly.

Max’s eyes turned to the stranger that stood in front of him; he could barely recognize the women he fell in love with. It wasn’t just her appearance that had changed; she had grown confident, maternal.

“I don’t want to see you, Max! Now leave and don’t

come back. When the babies are born, we'll sort something out with your mum – but not me, Max. I'm not letting you hurt me."

Somewhere in his alcohol muddled brain, Max noted the plural 'babies' and then dismissed it as a drunken mishear. Max locked eyes with Susan.

"Please, just give me five minutes... please. Just listen to what I have to say and then I will leave you alone." Her eyes said nothing, they were just a blank canvas with no emotion.

Susan stood for a moment examining him carefully. "Okay, you have five minutes and then you leave, Max. After that I don't want to see you again, do you understand?" She turned to Beth and Polly who stood side by side. "I need to speak to him... alone."

Polly looked at her and shrugged, "Okay, it's your call."

Susan turned and unlocked the door and Max followed behind her. "We'll be five minutes?" She shut the door behind and left Beth and Polly to sit in the car.

"You look like you need a coffee – maybe two or three!" She headed into the kitchen and Max followed behind her like a lost sheep in a strange land.

"Please can we just sit and talk for a minute?" his voice was shaky and husky.

She slammed the cups onto the kitchen counter. "Well? I'm listening, Max. Talk!"

Max sat, rubbing his hands together nervously. "Where do I start? I've gone over so many times what I wanted to say to you and now..."

"Just say what you have to say, Max, none of it is going to change my mind." She sharply cut him off mid sentence.

"What has happened to you, Susan? When did you become so cold, so emotionless?" his eyes studied her.

"The day I found you kissing her! That's *when* Max."

His head fell into his hands. "Nothing happened with her. Why won't you believe me? I wouldn't... couldn't ever look at another woman. I love you." He cleared his throat and sucked in the air. "She came to make trouble and she's succeeded. She wanted this to happen to us, Susan – she planned for this kind of carnage; it's what she does, she destroys me."

"What do I have to do to make you see that there's no one else but you? I can't eat or sleep, I can't concentrate on anything. I need you! I need our baby!" He begged.

"Babies!" her hand rested on her stomach and her eyes locked onto his. "It's twins, Max!"

The colour drained from his face – he had missed so much. "How? When did you find out...?" His hand stretched across the table to try and touch hers. "Please, baby."

Quickly, she pulled her hand away before he could touch it, one touch and that would be it. "Your five minutes are up, Max, it's time for you to go." She stood up signaling for him to leave.

"Just wait a minute," he grabbed hold of her wrist so tight that she could feel her heart rate increase.

"Max! Let go!" She tried to pull free. The butterflies danced at his touch. If she didn't get him out her feelings for him would return.

His grip loosened slightly.

"Max, we were a train wreck right from the start – we were destined to destroy one another. It's not going to work." She threw her hands up in the air and yanked herself from his grip.

"How can you say that? When you needed me I was always there – I still would be if you let me. I promise you that we can make this work, Susan… if you give it a chance."

Susan shook her head but Max hadn't finished, he still had the killer blow,

"You cheated on me and I forgave you... I did that because I love you. All I have ever done is love you."

Susan stood in front of the window looking out across the garden. "You don't see how it felt to stand there and watch your lips on another women, to watch your eyes sparkle for someone else."

"No? You want to know how I felt when I read your diary and discovered you'd spread your legs for a bloke you didn't even know the name of? It made me sick! Sick to the pit of my stomach."

Susan's hand came into sharp contact with his face. Her slap was hard and fast. "You bastard!" Her hand swung again. But this time he stopped it, grabbing her wrist with one hand and with the other, he pushed the hair off her face tenderly.

"I'm sorry. That was unforgiveable." His hand caressed the side of her cheek. The damned butterflies sang sweet love songs to him, pleading with him to touch her some more.

She turned her head away from him as a tear rolled down her face. "Its too late, Max, I have nothing left to give you."

Max moved closer to her, his lips touching her ear.

“Please, for the sake of our babies.” His hand rested on her belly. She nearly exploded with the feel of his fingers tracing tenderly over her stomach.

She turned and was nose to nose with him. The growing need to kiss him moved deep. “It’s for them I have to say no, Max!” His lips touched hers softly. The kiss was electrifying; ripples of energy spread through her body. For a moment she pulled away but the connection was too strong and the butterflies had won. Her hands ran through his knotted hair, pulling him further into her, his mouth melting with hers. She lost all her senses.

He held either side of her face in his hands. “Let me love you again, please. Just let me be yours.”

Susan fell to reality hard and fast. How could she let him kiss her? “Please leave - Now!” She shifted away from him and pointed towards the door.

“Come on, Susan. I know you felt it. We have a connection that runs deep.” It was too late there was nothing he could say to her to change her mind. He dipped his head and left out the door.

Chapter 16

"Hey, how are you feeling?" Polly's hand rested on Susan's shoulder; there was sympathy in her eyes. Susan hadn't said much in the three days since they came home and found Max sat on the doorstep. She hadn't felt anything since the butterflies were awoken by his touch.

Although Susan had not revealed what happened between them, Polly could see it in Susan's eyes that more had happened – whatever it was it had left its mark.

Susan turned. "Polly, I'm fine, really. You can stop asking me." She played around with the water in the sink, pretending to be busy. "I'm just… I almost believed him. Do you think I got it wrong?"

Polly shrugged. "You have been so strong these last few weeks, stronger than I have ever seen you before – you have to make your choices, Susan."

"I think I need to get away from this place – and from him. I need to get away from the memories."

Polly pulled the chair closer to her. "Well let's get away for a bit, just me and you, before these two come along and cause havoc." Polly's hand rested on Susan's stomach.

"No, Polly, I don't mean a break, I mean for good. I've decided to sell the house." This spur of the moment decision had lifted a weight off her shoulders and it felt good to take control once again.

Polly sat silent for a moment, thinking of how to respond. She'd become fond of this place and had made roots for herself here. It was just like Susan to spin everybody's world around and expect them all to stand firm. Although she loved Susan deeply, she also thought she could be a completely selfish bitch sometimes.

"Just like that, you want to leave. What about Beth?"

Susan stood and walked around the kitchen, her hand stroking the kitchen counter in agitation. "I don't know. I haven't really thought any of it through. I just think I need a fresh start."

More like running away, Polly thought.

"It's not going to really work with him living so close. I'm never going to be rid of the feelings when I know he's so close. I'm not saying that I'm going to miles away, I still want them to know their daddy and their grandma, I'm just saying this house, this stuff it's not... it's just stuff."

Polly sat shaking her head. "I think you need to sleep on this, really think it through before you make any rash decisions – these choices aren't just about you."

"I don't think sleep will change my mind." Susan said.

"What really happened the other day when you let him in, honey? You were doing fine until then."

"I... I don't know, he kissed me... I kissed him. It was instant between us, one minute we were talking, arguing, and for a split second nothing else mattered... the moment his lips touched mine, I lost myself." She paused through the sobs of tears that caught her breath. "What am I doing, Poll?"

Polly didn't have the answer. "I can't tell you what you need to do, you need to make this decision for yourself; you either follow your heart and take him back for the man he is, or you leave, move away, but if you do move, you must never look back, never doubt your decision, never think of him again – it's the only way you can truly be happy."

Susan smiled at her. She had a pounding headache and she rubbed the bridge of her nose between her fingers.

"Are you okay?" Polly asked.

"Yeah, I just need to go and have a lie down – do you mind?"

"No, head up and I'll bring you a cup of tea in about an hour or two."

Susan stumbled and grabbed the table to steady herself. She picked up the laptop on her way out of the room.

When she reached her room she pulled herself under the cover she turned the laptop on. She found what she was looking for in no time – a hotel... perfect for a few days away from every one. She followed the booking instructions online and booked in. She packed an overnight bag with a few clothes, enough to last at least a week. She had no idea how long she would be there but a week sounded long enough to finally decide what to do.

Once packed, Susan sighed with relief and tucked herself under the cover trying to fall into the world of sleep.

When Susan opened her eyes, the light from the morning sun appeared through the gaps in the blinds. She pulled herself from the bed and tiptoed to the bathroom, grabbing a few last minute bits that might be needed. Polly was still asleep, it was too early for her to be up. Confident she wouldn't be caught, she crept off to her room and grabbed the bag from under her bed. She looked at her watch and waited for the taxi by the door.

The note explaining that she had gone away for a few days was propped up against the kettle.

Her mobile beeped, indicating a text from the taxi guy.

She grabbed her bag, taking one last look behind her and breathing in every essence that filled the room; the heartache, the laughter and the dreams – she filled her lungs with them all before turning and leaving.

Max sat up in his bed; inside he was an empty space that would never be filled again. He hadn't been in touch with Susan since their kiss. He hated himself for pushing her to that point, but he had tried to make her see that they were both nothing without each other. He wanted her to know that he only had eyes for her – that no one would ever take her place. Half asleep, he took himself downstairs. For some reason he felt edgy, as if a terrible storm was about to break. He tried to ignore the feeling and headed into the kitchen. He opened the fridge and grabbed a nice cold beer. That was his only comfort these days. He pulled the cap of the top of the bottle and headed outside to sit on the back step. His thoughts turned to the day of the BBQ.

'Just one more try,' he thought to himself. Leaving the beer bottle on the step, he pulled himself up and down the garden and heading for the only place his heart rested, the only place he knew he would find her.

When he got to the beach, his heart skipped a beat as in the distance, close to the roaring waves, he caught glimpse of a shadow. "Go to her," the voice inside him whispered. His feet moved on their own. It was only as the sand coiled itself around his bare feet, that he realised he had forgotten to put anything on his feet. Max didn't care, he would walk naked if it meant that she would be here. His heart quickened as his feet took him closer and closer to the figure hugging herself on the beach. Closing his eyes, he let his body carry him the rest of the way. His lips were dry up from the anticipation. Would she open her arms and let him in? All he knew was this time he would never let her go. He needed her too much.

When he came within touching distance of the figure, he fell to his knees. Slowly he flickered his eyes open, only to shut them again. His hands pounded fist down onto the sand.

"NO!" he screamed. There was no figure, it had been a trick of his mind. She hadn't been waiting for him. Emptiness filled his soul, he would never be complete again; he would never know what it felt to feel love again. He sat for hours before pulling himself to his feet and forcing himself to leave. He promised himself that he would never come back again... ever.

When he reached the gate to the back garden of his mum's, he saw Polly standing at the back door.

"What are you doing here?" he hissed at her. "Has she sent you to give me more instructions about staying away from her?" He was beginning to get irritated by Polly's well-meaning interference.

Polly crossed her arms over her chest, she look worried. "Max I've come to ask for your help. She left this for me this morning." Polly passed him the letter. He took a moment to read it, his eyes scanning over the part about him over and over again.

"She's gone! Gone where?"

"That's just it, Max, I have no idea. She didn't give any indication that she was leaving and I don't know if she is coming back. She spoke about..." Polly paused, thinking for a moment about how much she should tell him. She shifted uncomfortably on her feet. "She spoke about you last night. She really spoke from the depth of her heart and when you… when you kissed her, you brought everything back to her. She is very confused about what she wants."

He ran his hand through his hair. "I don't know what you want me to do Polly. She made it very clear that I am nothing to her anymore. She told me she felt nothing for me." His fingers trained down his face. "I can't help you, I'm sorry, Polly. Now if you don't mind I need to get ready for work."

"Now you listen to me!" Polly's said sternly, her anger rising, "I'm not going to say I understand it, Max, but she feels everything for you. It's as if all her emotions are somehow tied to you; hate, love, anger, passion. She has been like a robot since you left. Ask your mum, Susan has shown hardly any emotion unless it was to do with you. She does loves you, Max – don't doubt that for a second."

Max slammed his fist against the door. "Then why is she doing this to me? If she feels the way you say she does, then why does she keep breaking me down this way?"

Hearing the commotion, Beth opened the door and seeing Polly she looked concerned.

"Is everything alright – are Susan and the babies alright?"

Polly shook her head. "No, Beth, sorry everything isn't alright."

Beth's hand flew to her mouth, "What's happened?"

"Susan has left."

"Left?"

Polly nodded, "I'm afraid so."

"But the babies are okay?"

"They're fine."

"Thank goodness for that."

"I'm here to tell Max that he has to do something."

"Of course he does," Beth agreed.

Beth's hand rested on his shoulder, "Max, if you don't do something soon to get her back then you will lose her forever. You need to find her and remind her of the love you share with each other."

Max sighed heavily. "But how do I do that when we don't know where she is?" An idea suddenly grabbed him. He turned to Polly and asked, "Where is her laptop?"

"It's at home, why?" Polly asked.

"I know one way we can try and find out where she is – through her browsing history. Come on!" He stood by Polly's car waiting for her to unlock the door. His hand shook as he gripped the handle.

As the car pulled up the drive to Susan's house, his heart stopped, remembering the last time he stepped into the house. He had been angry with himself for the way he had acted; the way he had lost his cool with her. Standing in the hall, he asked Polly to retrieve Susan's laptop; he was sure he'd find something on there that would indicate where she had gone. Polly rushed up the stairs as Max made his way to the living room. He stood in front of the window. His chest ached at the view; memories were attached to that view. Now they burned deep inside him like a dagger stabbing him over and over again.

"I found it." Polly broke his thoughts as she came rushing in the room holding the laptop in her arms. "I'll go and make us a drink." She left it resting on the table and went into the kitchen. Max sat rubbing his hands together waiting for it to load up. It didn't take long to access her history, scroll down it and find the name of a travel site.

"Bingo!" he chuckled to himself. "I knew she wouldn't have deleted her history."

"What have you found?" Polly called through from the kitchen.

"Online booking form."

Polly came to his side and handed him the cup of coffee. She looked over his shoulder at the screen, taking all the details in. "That's not that far away. You can be there in an hour, Max!" Her face slightly brightened.

"Whoa! What makes you think I'm going to go and chase after her... she went because she needs time and that's what I'm going to give her." Max shocked himself at the words he spoke – at one time he would have been on his bike right away, rushing towards her with the hope of holding her again.

Polly flipped her head to him. "Max, you need to go to her and make her see sense; yes she went to make her mind up, but you need to help her do that, because if you don't, she will leave and never come back. She has already spoken about selling this place and moving away. You have to make her see."

"She wants to sell this place!" She wouldn't, this is her home! This is her safe house, where she found herself – she would never sell it. Never!"

Polly took another sip of her coffee. "No, Max, you don't understand – this was your home together and she will never be happy here without you. You have to see that she would rather sell the last happy memory she has than be here without you. Doesn't that tell you that she is torn between her heart and her head?"

Max's breath fell heavy and sharp, the empty spaces filled his head. Once more, his fingers rubbed against his temple as he tried to decide what to do. His eyes travelled around the room. "Fuck it! I can't lose anymore than what I've lost already." His feet moved quickly as he set off out of the door. He had to pick up his bike first and then he could get on his way to bring back the women that held his heart in her hands.

Chapter 17

Susan stood on the balcony of her hotel room staring out at the first flickers of snow that fell. She didn't care how the cold bit at her skin, she couldn't feel it anyway; she couldn't feel anything. Every time she closed her eyes, his face appeared. Picking the coffee cup from the table, she stepped back into the room and sat on the end of the bed pulling her journal out of her bag. She started writing about how she felt. By the time she had finished the whole page was full of his name. When he had shown up at her house and he had kissed her he had unsettled her soul. Since that day she had been haunted in her sleep, reliving the same dream.

She lay down and tried to nap. Her hand resting over her tummy, cradling the two most important things in her life. Eventually she drifted off to sleep.

Max managed to sweet talk the receptionist of the hotel by pretending to be the deliverer of the bunch of roses he held in his hand. He smiled at the thought that the receptionist had probably only given him the room number because she fancied him, he knew that his smile was a secret weapon. But despite her being totally stunning, he had no interest in her. He was here for one reason, and he would't leave without her. Not this time.

As he exited the lift, he took a deep breath. He walked down the corridor, checking the numbers. When he found hers he stood outside the door, full of worry. He had hoped to clean himself up before another encounter with her, but hadn't had the chance; he ran his fingers through his hair, pushing the tangled mess off his face. His heart rate quickened as his hand came up to the door. He stopped before making contact. His gut snapped. *'Was he doing the right thing? Maybe she did just need time.'* The palms of his hands were sweating and trembling with nerves, something he had never had to worry about when he'd been around her before. He took a deep breath and knocked on the door. The wait felt endless.

"Just a moment," a frail voice whispered from behind the door.

Susan's eyes flickered open from her sleep. The sound of knocking at the door had startled her and her heartbeat was skipping all over the place. "Just a moment!" she croaked. She was shivering and she realized that she had left the balcony door open before falling asleep. She digged into the bottom of her bag and pulled out the only thing of Max's she had kept – his oversized hoodie. She breathed in his scent as she walked to the door.

Max held his breath as he heard her unlock the door. He could smell her body wash as soon as the door opened (a sexy berry smell that drove him wild every time he went in the bathroom when they lived together). As the door fully swung open, his eyes instantly met hers and it killed him…

Susan couldn't breathe when she saw the figure stood at the door; he had caught her totally off-guard. The butterflies in her stomach danced around and sang to her. Clutching at the hoodie, she walked backwards, inviting Max in.

Max cautiously strode forward, smiling when he saw

that she was wrapped up in his hoodie. His smile quickly shifted to concern. His true love now looked frail, skinny and very tired. His eyes roamed over her baby bump and he felt his heart hurt. He had missed touching her so much. Her eyes were brimming with tears. He held out his hand to touch her, but she shifted back from him like a timid animal. The room was silent. He cleared his throat… it's now or never.

"Susan, none of it was true." His voice was shaky and nervous. *Great way to start idiot.*

Susan didn't respond but she just stared deep into his eyes, like she was searching for something.

Max moved forward until his feet touched hers. His hand came up to her face and held it. She felt frozen. "Say something, Susan, please. I can't stand it anymore… anything - scream and shout at me if you want. Something…. anything!"

"Max…" The faintest sound came from her lips. "I have tried so hard to hate you but... but the more I have tried, the more it hurt in here." She clutched at her chest and closed her eyes.

Max pressed his hand to hers. He could feel her heart beating fast. "I'm here now, baby."

"I felt this moment happen a thousand time before I opened my eyes. I can't do any of this without you. I thought I could but I can't... I ... I need you!" The last words came out strong, almost begging. Her eyes were tightly shut as if fearful that should she open them then he might just disappear, and she might wake from her dream.

"Baby! Open your eyes. I'm here. I'm always here with you. Please look at me, Susan!" He had to make her see the truth.

Her eyes opened. Max stepped back. Where once they had been sparkling blue, they now looked like deep grey eyes, full of sadness, full of hurt. “Max….you’re really here?” Her hand traced the outline of his face. “I’m sorry, Max. I… I… didn’t want to push you away again I just…”

His finger pressed up against her lips. “None of it matters now. All that matters now is you three.” His hand covered the top her stomach. “I have missed you so much, baby.” He lent his forehead against hers, breathing her in. “God, you’re freezing, Susan, don’t move, baby.”

Susan stood with her arms wrapped around herself shaking uncontrollably. Max appeared behind her, wrapping her up in the thick blanket that was draped over the armchair.

He guided her to the bed and positioned the pillows and duvet in invitation.

“Please don’t go, Max. I’m so tired, lay down with me. Please don’t go again…” she pressed her cheek into the pillow, her eyes fighting to stay open.

Max lent over her caressing her cheek with the back of his hand. “Baby, I’m not going anywhere, I’m just going to order us some dinner and make you a warm drink. I’m never leaving your side again.”

Susan’s grip on his hand loosened. “Just hold me, Max. I need to be in your arms again... I need you to hold me.”

Max smiled and climbed under the cover with her, cradling her in his arms tightly. “I’m here.” He stroked her hair; it no longer trailed down her spine but stopped at her chin. “Susan why did you cut your hair?”

Susan gingerly looked up at him. “A fresh start I guess,

out with the old me in with the new."

Max kissed her forehead. "Well I love it! I loved old Susan but falling in love with new Susan sounds pretty good to me."

Susan giggled and pulled his face close to hers. "Max, I have missed you so much." Her lips touched his and the electricity came rushing back between them. She ran her fingers through his hair. Her eyes tired again, she fought the urge to sleep because she wanted to savour every moment with him.

Max stroked her back. "Go to sleep, baby. You really need to rest." He felt her body finally give in to the sleep it needed so much.

After making sure she'd fallen into a deep sleep he released her grip from around his waist and crept out of the bed into the bathroom. He stood staring at himself in the mirror, they both had a lot of talking they needed to do, he had to make her see that he wouldn't go anywhere again. Splashing cold water on his face, he heard a whimper from in the other room. Rushing in, he saw Susan tossing and turning on the bed. She was crying his name. "Baby, I'm here. Susan ssh, it's okay, I'm here." He curled his arm around her in reassurance. She stopped and wrapped her leg around his.

He laid his hand to rest on her belly and smiled when he could feel the babies moving around inside. Shuffling down the bed, he pressed his ear to her tummy and closed his eyes, shutting the whole world out and focusing on nothing but the two babies he treasured.

The sound of a knock at the door made Max shoot up in the bed; he must have drifted off to sleep. He climbed out of the bed and went to open the door. A very merry man wheeled a trolley in pushing it to the middle of the lounge area of the suit before leaving quietly out the door. Dinner.

Looking at Susan, he headed into the bathroom and turned the shower on. He examined himself in the mirror and trailed his hand over his tattoos. He still had so much explaining to do, so many things he wanted to say, but he needed to be here for her first. He wanted her back desperately but he didn't want her back unless she was sure. Pulling himself out his thoughts he stepped in the shower.

Susan woke, pulling her arms over her head to a stretch. She heard the sound of water running and smiled. *'He really is here!'* She threw the covers off the bed and waddled into the shower. She pulled the door open and climbed in behind him, fully clothed.

"Bloody Hell, Susan!" Max, laughed and wrapped his arms around her.

Susan squeezed him tighter. She didn't care about her clothes, all she cared for was him. "Max, you stayed. You really stayed." A tear fell from her eye, but it wasn't from sorrow, for the first time in a long time she was happy.

The water fell between them as his hands took hold of her face. "Susan, I told you I'm not leaving you and I meant it." His lips covered hers and he couldn't control the power behind the kiss. "God you taste so good!" He pulled her hoodie and vest top over her head and his eyes fell to her swollen breasts. A cheeky seductive smile appeared on his face.

"OH MY GOD! Max what is that?" her hand covered his upper arm. Max looked down at her hand, resting his own on top of hers. He moved it from the tattoo to around his waist, pulling her in closer. “Look closely here.” His fingers pointed to something written in the eagle’s wing.

“Oh, Max!” her hand flew around his neck and she kissed him hard. “I can’t believe you got a tattoo with my name on. Are you mad?”

He nodded his head. “Yep, madly in love.” He returned his lips to hers, pulling her closer. His hands cupped her heavy breasts, circling her nipples, causing her to feel tight concentric rings of pleasure. She moaned into his mouth and he broke away with a laugh. “Come on, baby you need to eat.”

She looked at him, her eyes glittering, “Well, Max, that’s a bit forward,” she said slapping his bottom.

He stroked her cheek – I mean, dinner!”

“Oh,” she said pouting.

Max stepped out off the shower and grabbed two towels off the rail. He wrapped one around his waist and helped Susan out before wrapping her up in a towel.

“Come on, baby, the food is getting cold. When they had both finished getting dressed they walked hand in hand to the table. Max pulled a chair out for her and walked around the table to sit opposite her.

“Max, can we talk?”

Susan kept her eyes on the food in front of her not wanting to stare into those eyes.

Max stared up at her. “What do you want to talk about, Susan?”

“Everything!” Susan threw the napkin onto the table. “Max we need to talk about where we go from here. I can’t go back to that house without you… I can’t pretend I’m strong enough to get through it all because I'm not! I need you!"

Max took her hand, his breathing was heavy. "You don't have to go back without me, not if you don't want to. You know how I feel about you."

"Max, I love you and I can't spend another moment without you in my life. We waited too long to find each other. Please come home." She pulled her chair around next to his and clasped her hand close to his chest.

"I'm already there, baby!"

Susan stared deep into his eyes. She had so much to tell him but she just couldn't find the words. "Max, we have to be completely honest with each other from now on, no secrets. I can't go back and do this all over again – I have too much to lose."

Max ran his fingers through his hair pausing for a moment. "Whatever you want to know baby I will tell you. I have nothing to hide from you – no more secrets. But I know you have something you need to know, so ask me.

Susan huffed under her breath, how did he know what she wanted to know?

"Okay, who is Isabelle to you? Who were you, Max? I mean when you were growing up."

He shuffled uncomfortably. "I think I'm going to need a drink first!" Max walked over to the mini-bar and poured himself a double whiskey. He threw it down his throat and poured another. "Come and sit down, baby."

Susan sat next to him and curled around him, playing with the buttons on his shirt. "Max, listen," she turned to face him, "You don't have to tell me if you don't want to, I understand."

Max took hold of her chin and stroked her lips with his thumb. “Susan, you told me everything about your past right from the start and I want to tell you, I just don’t want you to be ashamed of me when you hear it.” He had always been ashamed of his time with Izzy but he had to make sure that he shared everything with Susan if he were to ever get to go home with her.

He took another sip of his drink and cleared his throat. “When me and Izzy first got together, she was… she was very full on. We were young and I was… I thought I was in love with her. I would do anything to keep her happy. She started to control me. I mean, I lost touch with most of my mates and I hardly spoke to my mum and dad. I was never allowed near any other girls, not unless she authorized it.” Max stopped and took another sip.

Susan swallowed hard. “Max you really don’t have to go on if you don’t want…”

His finger came up to her lips again. “No! I need to tell you. After months of her controlling me, I lost it one night. We got into a massive fight but she seemed to be enjoying the fact that she drove me to the edge. She had actually enjoyed the fact that I lost it with her. FUCK! I hate saying the words.”

He dipped his head not wanting to look into her eyes. “The first time we argued she became wild, it turned her on that I was angry with her and I mean sex with her wasn’t making love – it wasn’t how it is with…”

Susan shook her head and he read the message loud and clear.

“I mean it was… it was wild but it was nothing more than… fucking.” He dropped his voice with shame, “And I loved it. When we argued, she would drive me wild with desire. She quickly learned that she could make me do absolutely anything if it meant I could screw her after, and so she started treating me like her slave. It didn't happen overnight, she was a skilled manipulator. By the end of it, I had to beg at her feet before she would touch me!"

Susan sat with her eyes wide. She was desperately not trying to cry. Her flesh crept.

He looked out towards the window. His voice was merely more than a whisper, "And I fucking loved it, Susan. I mean it turned me on that I had to beg her for it. What kind of man does that make me?" He stood up and walked to the balcony door – he needed air; he couldn't breathe. Max shook his head.

"Are you alright," she asked.

He shook his head, "No, I feel sick! I hate myself. Underneath all of this, I'm a monster; an animal! Then you came along and everything about you made me see the man I wanted to be – the man I could be. I couldn't pull myself away from you, even after everything you told me, I just couldn't leave you because I know that I belong to you."

Silence fell between them. They spent minutes looking at the snow falling outside the window. Eventually, Susan spoke, "I love you. More than anything!"

Max pulled his phone from his pocket flicking through his songs; he found the one he wanted and pressed play. "Every time I listen to this song I think of you."

Susan sat listening to the words and tears appeared. "What song is this Max?"

"Shania Twain *'It's in the way.'* Listen."

Susan listened to the lyrics. "It's beautiful." Suddenly

Susan tensed and Max jumped up from the chair. “What’s wrong, baby? What is it?” Worry washed over his face.

Giggling she took his hand and placed it on her stomach. “It’s fine, Max, they’re just waking up. Feel!”

Max touched the spot she guided it to; he could feel hands and feet kicking to get out. He had never felt anything as magical in his life. “Just waking up?”

“Yeah, for the past couple of weeks they both get really active at night. I spend all night in bed talking to them.”

“Can we go home, Susan?”

Max lent his head down to her belly his lips softly touching. “Hello, you two. I’m your daddy,” he whispered.

Chapter 18

Four weeks of wedding planning later.

"Come on, Susan, you need to get up. We'll be late!" Polly shouted up the stairs. Susan refused to move, she curled herself back into a ball and pulled the cover over her head. "Susan, you get out that bed or so help me, I'll drag you out – pregnant or not!"

Susan threw back the covers and groaned. "Fine, I'm up! But I want a coffee when I get down there! Caffeinated!" Stretching herself out, she started the long process of getting out of bed. Max usually helped her but he wasn't allowed to stay at home last night. It was 'bad luck'. Polly and Beth both insisted on him staying at his childhood home. Pulling her legs out first, and slowly lifting her body out, she then rushed to the bathroom – the babies playing havoc with her bladder. "You two could at least wait for me to get out the bed before bouncing on my bladder" she said, looking down at her tummy.

"Here she is!" Party poppers exploded around the kitchen when she walked in. Polly jumped up and down with excitement. "Today is the day!"

Susan slumped down in the chair and sipped her coffee. "I know what day it is, Polly. It's the day I walk along that beach looking like the beached whale!"

"Don't be silly, Susan, you will look amazing!" Beth placed a reassuring hand on her shoulder.

They had managed to plan everything out for the

wedding in time but Susan had grown more and more self-conscious about her figure. She couldn't see her feet anymore and she looked enormous. Everyone told her she looked perfect, but nothing made her feel better.

"I'm going for a shower." Susan stood up and made her way to the bathroom. Passing the nursery, she smiled at all the finishing touches they had added over the last few weeks. Two cots sat side-by-side, one with pink blankets and one with blue. She only had a matter of weeks left before she would go in hospital and leave with her babies.

When she finished in the shower she went downstairs to a house full of people, that included a hairdresser, a make-up artist and a dressmaker, which Beth had suggested in case the dress needed any last minute touches to it.

"Okay let's start on your hair!" Polly sat her down in the kitchen chair, chatting away to the hairdresser. Susan sat playing with her phone, not listening to anyone around her. Max said he would text her as soon as he woke up.

The hairdresser pulled and tugged at her hair for the next half hour before stepping back to examine her masterpiece. "It's gorgeous!" Polly jumped up, clapping her hands together.

Susan's phone buzzed on the table. Quickly picking it up, she opened the message.

Good morning, Mrs. Tyler x love you x

Smiling she texted him back.

Not Mrs. Tyler yet! And I love you too. Can't wait to c u xxx

She placed the phone back on the table, smiling as the beautician started on her makeup. Her phone buzzed a second time.

I'll be waiting!

Polly grabbed the phone off her. "Susan, you know you can't speak to him, it's bad luck!" She put the phone in her handbag.

"Poll, it was a quick text and, technically, I didn't talk to him." Susan giggled as the women tickled her face with the brush.

Beth sat at the other end of the table watching Susan laughing, "You are beautiful, Susan."

Susan stood and followed the dressmaker up the stairs. The butterflies in her stomach danced around and she tried to push them aside. Every night since Max had fallen asleep talking to their babies, he woke in the morning with her wrapped in his arms. Perfect didn't come much better.

As the dressmaker helped Susan into her dress, she felt her cheeks redden. "I look stupid, I knew I would!" Susan slumped on the end of her bed with her head in her hands.

The women came close taking hold of Susan's hands. "No, you look like an angel. Perfect. Look!" She led Susan to the full-length mirror on the wall.

Susan didn't recognize the reflection, it wasn't her. The woman standing in front of the mirror looked like a goddess, her body ripe with life and hope. She smiled at the dressmaker as she left the room. "Thank you!" she whispered. Susan turned from side to side in front of the mirror, taking all of her image in. 'One thing missing' she thought to herself, digging in the drawers for the necklace Max had given her. Stepping back she took one more look. She took one deep breath and opened the bedroom door taking her time down the stairs so not to trip over the dress. As she reached the bottom, she brushed herself down waiting for a response from the people watching. "Well, will I do?"

Polly's hand came up to her mouth, she was fighting back tears. "Oh my god, Susan, you look... I can't even describe. You look amazing!"

Beth stood in the doorway unable to stop tears running down her cheeks.

"Beth, don't cry, you're making your make up run."

"Come on, your man is waiting." Polly tugged at Beth and Susan leading them out the door and to the car.

Max stood under the canopy next to Dillon waiting. He checked his watch every few seconds. "Chill, man! She will be here. Polly just texted to say they'd set off." Dillon reassured Max, and slapped him on the back. Dillon had been a bit of a strange choice for best man, but in truth there wasn't really anybody else, besides, Dillon and Polly seemed to be making a go of things, and there was evidence to suggest that it might all get a little serious.

He had spent the whole week watching the weather channel, making sure that the snowstorm would stay clear today. Susan had been adamant she wanted the wedding at the beach but wouldn't wait for better weather. They had a canopy erected over the pagoda in an attempt to keeping most of the cold sea wind off them, but he still worried the rain wouldn't hold. The weatherman had forecast that a huge winter storm would be heading their way over the next couple of days. 'Just don't rain yet' he thought to himself looking up to the clouds.

Max kept his eyes on the steps, watching and waiting. "Could they take any longer? I'm dying here."

Just then Polly waved from the top of the steps, signaling Dillon to play the music. Max's heart stopped, as he waited for Polly to walk down the steps holding her flowers. Shania Twain played in the background. It was the song that had told her he really loved her.

"Man, she looks hot!" Dillon whispered to Max.

Max flipped his head and glared at Dillon.

"I mean Polly! Relax, Man." Dillon held his hands up and they shared a much-needed laugh.

Max's attention turn back to the steps. His eyes locked with Susan and he lost his breath for a second. His legs wobbled and he almost fell. His eyes never moved from her. Her long white lace dress flowed in the cool ocean breeze and the wind ruffled the fur throw around her shoulders. He watched as her bare toes touched the sand. (Only his crazy girl would go shoeless with a threat of a winter storm) Curls fell on her face and snowdrops laced her hair. The low winter sun created a shimmering halo around her.

Susan felt the butterflies as soon as his hand touched hers; no words could describe the feelings she felt. As the song finished, they turned hand in hand to the registrar, their eyes never parting. Polly and Beth took a seat next to Dillon and they watched patiently as both Max and Susan struggled to find the words they wanted to say.

Max held his breath as the words 'I do' came from her lips. The only women he ever loved had become his wife; he took her head in his hands and their lips touched. Waves crashed onto the sand salty breeze flew. Max didn't care, he didn't want the kiss to ever end. He turned to Beth and Polly; they were both uselessly romantic, with tears in their eyes. They were both so happy that Max and Susan couldn't help but giggle with delight.

As the music started again, Susan took Max's hand. They would never be apart again. With Max and Susan in one car and Polly, Beth and Dillon in another, they all headed back to Susan's for a small celebration. Everyone had wanted a fancy reception but Susan had put her foot down and decided on just the five of them and a small gathering at her house. It's the only place she wanted to be in such a fragile state; the babies had taken all her strength and she just wanted to relax and spend her day with the people she loved.

The house was full of flowers and the table had been set with borrowed vintage china and linen that had once been Beth's mothers. Beth had made enough cakes and sandwiches for a reception of twenty.

Max watched every move Susan made; his eyes never left hers until Beth stood up and cleared her throat before announcing, "Hey, I know it's only us but I'd still like to say a few words and raise a glass. I'd like to say how proud I am of you both and I know, Susan, that your mother and father would be overwhelmed at the amazing women you have turned into. You are going to last a lifetime together."

"Mom!" Max turned and pulled his teary-eyed mum in for a hug. "I love you, Mom!"

Polly stood and tapped the side of her champagne glass. "Well, I think if we are doing speeches I'd also really like to say something."

"Polly," Susan smiled, "you really don't have to!"

Polly looked directly at Susan. "When I met you I thought you would never find your happy ending. I thought you were lost forever, but then after all the tears and heartache…" a tear trickled down her cheek. "I've seen you grow in confidence, I've seen you passionate, loving, and caring. I've seen you fight for what you want and with you by her side, Max, I know she will have a life filled with love and happiness."

Susan couldn't control the tears. They all lifted their glasses cheering. Max took Susan's hand and led her into the living room. Polly pressed play and *'From this moment'* echoed in the background. Max wrapped his arms around her waist and led her in a slow dance. They couldn't take their eyes off each other; nothing in the world mattered but that moment. "I love you, Mrs. Taylor." His lips caressed her forehead.

"I love you too, Mr Taylor."

"Here, take a seat for a bit your feet must be aching?" Max guided her to the sofa and pulled her feet up over her knees. He rubbed the soles of her feet and they both giggled as they watched Dillon dancing with Polly and Beth. "How are you feeling, baby?" he whispered, removing a wisp of hair from her face.

"I'm the happiest I've ever been, Max." Susan couldn't stop smiling.

He lent in closer to her ear. "I mean are you tired? Do you need a lie down or anything?"

Max I'm fine!"

Polly danced over to the two of them, pulling Max up off the couch. "Come on, Max, you owe me a dance."

Beth took a seat next to Susan. "I meant what I said, Susan, your parents would be so proud of you."

"Do you really mean it?"

"Oh, sweetie, yes I mean it. You are so much like your mother, but you have your father's fight. Even in the dark your smile shines through." She touched Susan's cheek.

"I can't remember anything about them, you know? No matter how much I try." Beth shadowed her pain. "How long did you know them?" Susan asked.

Beth paused for a moment trying to remember a time that she didn't't know Susan's parents – it was as if they had been part of her growing-up. When they had died, Beth had been left bereft. "I knew your mother from school and I first met your father I when they became a couple at seventeen. They were such a lovely couple and they loved each other very much." Beth took a breath. "They also loved you very much..."

"I love you, Beth. I'm so glad that you are in my life."

The two of them sat watching the others smiling and laughing. Max hopped over to Beth and took hold of her hand. "May I have this dance, Mom?" He gave a wink at Susan. "I'll be back for you in a little while."

Susan smiled as the babies kicked around in her tummy. She had finally got everything she ever wanted... she had finally become a wife to the man who had always owned her heart, and she would soon become a mother. She was surrounded by people that loved her.

"How are my two little munchkins doing? Aunty Polly is going to spoil you two rotten!" she said, flopping down on the sofa next to her.

"You made me jump!" Susan turned laughing at her. "You're drunk!"

"Nope!" Polly shook her head and giggled. "Okay maybe just a little bit. I think I may need to go home soon."

Dillon walked over and pulled Polly to her feet. “Let’s get you home, Missy.” He winked at her and Susan knew exactly what was on the agenda.

“Dillon, I think you’ve had a little bit too much to drink to be taking anyone home, don’t you? I’ll drive you all back.” Susan stood and headed for the door, pushing her swollen feet into her trainers.

“Baby, what you doing? You should be resting. Max walked over and grabbed hold of her arm

“I’m fine, I won’t be long.” Susan took Polly’s coat and held it up for her.

“Susan, we can walk, it’s only ten minutes away. You really don’t need to drive us, honest you get some rest.”

“Whoa! Will you all stop fussing, I need some fresh air anyway. I’ll be fine. Like you said, it’s only ten minutes away. Now come on you three, let’s get you all tucked up in bed shall we.” Susan shook her head laughing. “Don’t worry, Max, I’ll be back in no time – then you can take me to bed!” she pressed her lips against his cheeks.”

Susan rushed to the car not wanting to get wet from the splatters of rain that fell. She climbed behind the wheel of Polly's car, pushing the seat back as far as it would go before starting the engine. “Belts please!” She shot a look behind her at Polly and Dillon slumped in the back their heads lolling on each other. They both huffed, buckling the seatbelts into place. Beth sat in the front.

As the car pulled up on Beth's drive, Susan looked over her shoulder and chuckled. “Look at those two, fast asleep!”

Beth shook Polly’s leg. “Come on sleepy-head!”

Susan unfastened her seatbelt and was just about to

climb out of the car when Beth pulled her back into her seat and clung tight to her neck. "I had a wonderful day today, Susan. Thank you for letting us be a part of your day."

Susan couldn't hold back her tears.

They shambled out of the car and waved enthusiastically from the door step, laughing as Beth struggled to find her keys.

She sent Max a text telling him she was setting back off and threw the phone on the passenger seat before starting the engine up again. She waited until the three of them had got through the door before heading off.

The rain was falling heavily. When she stopped at the traffic lights, she flicked the radio on singing away to the music, when the lights hit green she started moving forward. A sharp pain shot across her stomach. Susan gripped the steering wheel as tightly as she could but the pain was too much and it crippled her. The rain thrashed across the windscreen and she couldn't see anything in front of her. All at once she started to panic.

With one hand over her belly, she muttered to herself, "It's okay, babies we're nearly home." Then another sharp pain ripped across her belly, this time it was followed by a gush as her waters broke.

She wrapped both her hands around her tummy, loosing complete control of the car and praying for the safety of her babies. Her eyes closed in agony as her body jolted to the sound of the car crunching into another car. Everything went black…

Chapter 19

In the distance tiny lights flickered. She felt Max's presence. She tried shouting out but no words came out. Everywhere hurt. She could hear sirens in the distance. "Just a little longer," she gargled. She could taste iron in her mouth. "Just hold on a little longer, babies."

The blackness came at her again. "Max!" She couldn't understand why he didn't respond.

"Hello! Hello! Miss, are you okay?" She heard the faint sound of a man's voice. "Its okay we'll get you out, just hold on!" The voice spoke again. "We need to get her out of there now…"

Lights flashed all around her, "Please save them…don't let them die…" her eyes closed again. A faint voice echoed through the car.

Visions flashed forward like movies in her head. Max was holding hands with a little girl, her blond curls wild in the wind.

The vision vanished. The pain was too much, the iron in her mouth was making her feel sick and her head hurt, but it was nothing compared to the pain ripping through her tummy. In the distance she heard the sound of shouting.

Max took another look at his watch. He was getting worried, she should be back by now – it had been twenty minutes since she had texted to say that she was on her way home. Picking up his phone he tried phoning again only this time it went straight to voicemail. Grabbing his keys he left the house and walked to the end of the street to see if he could see her. Something was wrong.

As he reached the end he could see blue flashing lights in front of him. His gut was hit hard. He screamed out from deep inside and he ran. The car was upside down in the ditch. “SUSAN!” he screamed. Strong arms pulled him back.

“Please, Sir, step back. Do you know who is in the car?”

“It’s… it’s my wife! Is she… please tell me she is okay!” Max ran his hands through his hair and he dropped to his knees on the floor.

“Please, Sir, I need you to remain calm and let us help her. We believe she has gone into labour and we are concentrating on getting her out in the safest way possible. We have given her some pain-killers but she keeps slipping in and out of consciousness. Do you think you could talk to her and try to keep her awake while the fire crew get her out?”

Max nodded and moved towards the car with the help of the police officer. He knelt down and took hold of Susan’s hand. “Susan, baby, please open your eyes.” His heart was accelerating and he thought that he might pass out. “Baby, open your eyes. It’s Max – please open your eyes. I need you to do that for me, baby.”

“Max?” her words were shaky.

He tightened his grip on her hand and pushed her tangled, bloody hair off her face. “Yes, baby, I’m here. Please hold on a little longer.”

Her eyes struggled to open. Tears streamed down her face.

Sir, can you just move aside, please," the paramedic laid the stretcher out on the floor as the fire crew prepared to lift her out of the car.

Susan felt Max loosen his grip. "NO!" she screamed out. "Please don't let go. Please don't leave me."

"Baby, I'm right here." Max stood helplessly by, watching her scream out in pain as they fastened her into the stretcher.

Sharp pains shot across her stomach, she couldn't move. "AH! It hurts!" she sobbed. "Please save them!"

"Tell me she is going to be okay?" Max couldn't control his tears and he couldn't stop thinking about how much pain she was in. As the doors shut on the ambulance, he took hold of her hand.. "Its okay, baby, I'm right here."

"Max, I can't see you. Please, I'm scared…" Her vision went black and not even his voice could bring her back.

He sat in the waiting room waiting for news, looking down at his hands covered in her blood.

"Max!" Beth shouted as she came running up the corridor. Polly followed behind "Oh my God, Max! Have they said anything?" Polly asked.

Max sat with his head in his hands. "Mom…. I…I… can't lose her." Beth sat cradling his head in her arms as his body shook violently. "What am I going to do mom? What if I lose them?"

"Ssh, Max, you're not going to lose them. Don't give up." A trail of ugly black mascara ran down Beth's face.

Polly and Beth sat either side of him. He felt himself falling to pieces. "I can't sit here and do nothing!" he said, standing up and pacing up and down the corridor. He was waiting for someone to come – an angel of mercy. Seconds turned into minutes, minutes turned into an hour and still no one came.

"I'm going to go and get a coffee. Do you want one?" Polly gingerly stood up and wiped the tears from her eyes.

Max shook his head. He couldn't think of such earthly things now; not when he was in danger of losing his precious babies and the woman that held his heart.

"Come on, I'll walk with you," said Beth. "I need to exercise my legs." She turned to Max, "Will you be okay for a minute or two, son?"

Max shook his head and stared up at the ceiling. His chest hurt and he couldn't breathe properly. He watched the two women walk down the corridor and through the swing doors arm in arm. When he was sure they were no longer in hearing, he walked to the wall and punched it hard, so hard that the plaster cracked under his knuckles. "Fuck!" he hissed. He pulled at his hair and turning, slid down the wall and dropped to the floor hard. He didn't feel it. He rested his head on his knees and tried to catch his breath. "Please, God. Please don't let them die."

Polly returned, slowly approaching him and settling down next to him. She pushed a cup of coffee in his direction. "Max! She's going to be okay."

He lifted his head and turned in her direction. All the colour had drained from his face. "How the hell can you be sure of that, Polly?"

Her hand touched his. "Because it's Susan; she's fought all her life to get what she has and she won't give up on it now. Trust me."

Susan's eyes shot open; she lay in the hospital bed opening her mouth to speak but no words came out. She pulled the cover back and felt for the floor with her feet. There was no pain. She felt empty inside. She cried out for Max but the room was silent. She could hear a faint cry on the other side of the door – it sounded like babies crying. She dashed over to the door but it was locked and she couldn't get out. Her fists pounded uncontrollably on the door but she was trapped. The more she hammered on the door, the more they cried.

She fell to the floor sobbing. She could hear footsteps outside and the crying stopped. She could hear a man's voice... His voice. She stood up on her tiptoes and peered through the glass. She could see him in the distance, even with his back turned to her, she knew it was Max. He held something bundled in his arms. Her heart jumped in her chest. "Max!" she screamed, "I'm in here!" He turned but he didn't take his eyes from the bundle in his arms. "It's okay, Hope, daddy's here." Tears tricked down his face and landed on the tiny baby wrapped in a blanket.

'Hope!' she whispered. It had been the name they had chosen together the night before…

Another cry came from a second cot in the room and Max turned his attention to it. Susan banged as hard as she could on the glass but he could not hear. As he bent his head down into the cot, the crying stopped. "Ssh, Jacob!" A tiny collection of fingers wrapped around his finger.

Frantically she ran around the room, throwing the chair at the door and kicking and screaming in hope of him hearing her.

"Ssh, child!" A voice came from the corner of the room.

A woman sat on the end of the bed. She was beautiful, an angelic vision in white. "It's no use, he can't hear you, Susan."

"Who are you?" she asked tremulously.

The woman shook her head. "You know who I am. I'm here to help you."

Susan backed away from her. She knew that if she let this woman too close, then she would never hold her babies in her arms – she would never go home.

Three hours had passed and Max never moved off the floor. At last they heard the swing doors go and through bleary eyes he could make out a figure? Polly and Beth reached to comfort each other on the seats. A man, dressed in theatre robes, his mask dangling from his ear, walked over to them and cleared his throat waiting for Max to stand. "Mr Taylor?"

Max nodded but he couldn't find the strength to lift himself up. He saw from the expression on the surgeons face that things were not good.

"Mr Taylor. You'll be relieved to know that we managed to deliver both babies safely..." the surgeon hesitated and Max felt his throat turn to sand.

"W…what about Susan? Is she…Did she make it?"

The doctor's face contorted as he choose his words carefully. He coughed and cleared his throat. "You have to understand that she sustained quite a serious head injury and a broken leg, but, apart from that, she was very lucky. We believe she went into labor causing her to lose control of the car…"

"So, she is okay? Can I see her now?" Max ran his fingers through his hair.

"If you'd like to follow me I'll take you to her. Now before you go in I need to warn you that she hasn't regained consciousness just yet and she is very wired up. We can't quite understand why she's not come round yet, but it's not unheard of for it to take a little while. We are waiting for her scan results but up to yet there is no reason that we can ascertain."

"What do you mean *'no reason'*? You said she had sustained a head injury, is she in a coma?" Worry flashed over his face – he could still lose her.

The doctor smiled apologetically, "I'm afraid she seems to have given up. It's like she's gone somewhere else for a while. We did everything we could and it's now down to her."

Max stood in the doorway afraid to enter. He could hear the machines before he could see them. "Doctor, tell me the truth, do you think she is going to make it?" Max felt her slipping between his fingers.

The surgeon sighed heavily, "That is out of our control now." He pushed open the door and let Max through, "I'll leave you for a while. I'll be on rounds in about an hour." He turned and walked away down the corridor.

Max took a deep breath as he approached the bed. He took hold of her hand. "Susan, baby!" he lent over and whispered into her ear. "Baby, you need to wake up. We need to go and see our babies together. You can wake up now. They need their mummy."

He heard Beth gasp behind him. Her hand rested on his shoulder. "Max!"

"It's okay, Mom, she will wake up. She has to." He looked over his shoulder at Polly. "It's okay, Polly, I know she will be fine. Like you said, she will fight this."

Polly approached playing with the bottom of her top. She perched on the bed and took hold of her other hand. "Come on, honey, you have two babies that need feeding. You've got to wake up, I'm not babysitting! I'm rubbish with babies." Max gave her a smile as the three of them sat talking to her as though she was awake.

Time passed and there was a tap at the door. A head popped around the corner. "I hope you don't mind?" the women stepped into the room wheeling a crib "I just thought that you would like to meet these two!"

Beth jumped up, "Oh my! Can I?" she moved forward stretching out her arms.

The nurse laughed kindly. "Of course you can. Go ahead, I'll pop back in half an hour to take them back up to the baby unit."

"Oh, Max come here, they are gorgeous!" Beth snuggled one of the tiny babies up in her arms. "You have your mummy's eyes, yes you do, don't you?"

Polly bent down and carefully picked up the other baby.

Max sat still on the bed, refusing to look at them. How could he look at them without her? "I can't. I can't see them until she wakes up – we are meant to look at them together. We are meant to meet them together. Take them out, please, we're not ready."

"Max!" Beth said, shocked. "You can't turn away from them. They need you just as much as she does. How do you think she would feel if she found out you turned your back on them? I don't care if you're not ready to meet them, they're ready to meet their daddy."

"You don't understand," he said, "Please, just take them away." Max felt his gut snap; it killed him inside not to look at them, but he couldn't bring himself to move from her side. He couldn't bring himself to love them without her.

"You don't mean that!" Polly shouted furiously from the back of the room.

Max stood up. "I can't... I just can't. I… I want you both to leave, right now!"

Polly carried the baby over to him. "Look at your, son Max! Look at him. He needs you." She held him out for Max to hold. "Don't tell me you don't feel anything."

Max tried to look away, but the baby let out a little mewl and he couldn't help himself. He stared into the tiny blue eyes – her eyes - and he stroked over the thick brown hair on the tiny head. His face twisted with pain and sorrow. Tears started to brim his eyes.

"I don't…I don't know what to do. I'm sorry." He fell into the chair. Polly bent down and passed the baby into his arms. Beth walked over carrying the other baby and carefully placed her into his other arm, which took a certain amount of awkward readjustment. She nudged Polly's elbow signaling for them to take their exit.

Max couldn't take his eyes of the two strangers in his arms. "Daddy's here!" he whispered. When he heard the door click shut, he couldn't hold back the tears. "Susan, open your eyes – I need you to see how beautiful they are."

He sat back in the chair sobbing uncontrollably, his heart torn between his children and the love of his life.

"I can't do this without you."

He stood up and laid the babies at Susan's side. "We are going to be right here when you open your eyes, baby. All three of us."

The end

Almost.

"Daddy, Daddy!" Four year old Hope ran along the beach towards Max. She threw her arms around him. "Jacob won't let me play with Granny." Tiny tears fell over her cheek as she pointed down the water.

"Oh, sweetie, it's okay." Max tenderly ran his hands under her eyes, wiping away her tears. "Let's go and get some ice-cream, yeah?" He stood up, holding his hand out for her.

"Daddy, should we get Aunty Powy one too?" The little girl danced along beside him, her hand wrapped in his.

Max laughed. "Yeah, we can get Aunty Polly one too, and Uncle Dillon."

"No, he smells funny!" She let go of his hand. "Look, daddy, I can ballerina!" She danced around him, twirling around.

"You mean you can dance like a ballerina, Hope?" He crossed his arms over his chest and watched as she danced.

She stopped, stomping her foot. "That's what I said, daddy, I can ballerina."

With a handful of ice-creams, he walked down the beach towards Beth who sat building sand castles with Jacob. "Hey, Jacob, let Hope play with granny too!"

"But daddy, she just wants to do dancing," the tiny voice protested.

Beth giggled, looking over her shoulder at Max.

"Here you go, you two." He passed the ice-creams over to Polly and Dillon.

"Thanks, Max – I think this little one is craving ice cream. I'm eating it by the bucket load." She laughed, pressing her hand over her belly.

Two hands pressed over his eyes and he felt his heart skip and dance at the feel of her touch. Both children fell into fits of giggles. He turned around to kiss her, but Susan ran off across the beach laughing. As Max caught up with her, he pulled her onto the sand. He kissed her hard. "I love you, Susan."

She took hold of his face with both hands examining his expression. "Take me home and show me how much Max..."

ABOUT HAZEL ROBINSON

WWW.HAZELROBINSON.WEEBLY.COM

"I've always had a passion for reading but over the last several years it has become an obsession, a few months ago I decided to put fingers to keys to keyboard (or pen to paper!) and write "Something Missing", a story I've had hidden away in the back of my mind for a long time."

Hazel lives in the small town of Rishton in Lancashire. England, with her husband, three children, two cats, dog, rabbit and lizard. She fills her days dashing between school runs, pets and housework and at night she comes to life either writing or watching
her favorite program '*Supernatural*' (Yes, she is obsessed)

Her road to writing started with a love for paranormal romance novels, and after finding a passion for tragic romance she set out on the mission to share her story. After long nights writing, and a lot of '*Supernatural*' episodes, she is finally ready to share 'Something Missing'. Hazel loves nothing better than sitting with a cup of tea, a chocolate biscuit and a good book.

6327838R00119

Printed in Great Britain
by Amazon.co.uk, Ltd.,
Marston Gate.